I0534700

Marry Me for Real, COWBOY

CAVANAGH COWBOYS ROMANCE - 1

VALERIE COMER

Greenwords Media

Copyright © 2020 Valerie Comer
All rights reserved.
Digital ISBN: 9781988068589
Paperback ISBN: 9781988068596

No part of this publication may be reproduced or transmitted for commercial purposes, except for brief quotations in printed or electronic reviews, without written permission of the author.

This is a work of fiction set in a fictional western Montana. Businesses and locations are used fictitiously. Any resemblance to actual persons, living or dead, is coincidental.

Cover Art © 2020 Lynnette Bonner, www.indiecoverdesign.com.

Cover image from Deposit Photos

Holy Bible, New International Version®, NIV® Copyright ©1973, 1978, 1984, 2011 by Biblica, Inc.® Used by permission. All rights reserved worldwide.

First edition, GreenWords Media, 2020

Valerie Comer Bibliography

Urban Farm Fresh Romance

0. Promise of Peppermint (ebook only)
1. Secrets of Sunbeams
2. Butterflies on Breezes
3. Memories of Mist
4. Wishes on Wildflowers
5. Flavors of Forever
6. Raindrops on Radishes
7. Dancing at Daybreak
8. Glimpses of Gossamer
9. Lavished with Lavender
10. Cadence of Cranberries
11. Joys of Juniper

Christmas in Montana Romance

1. More Than a Tiara
2. Other Than a Halo
3. Better Than a Crown

Farm Fresh Romance

1. Raspberries and Vinegar
2. Wild Mint Tea
3. Sweetened with Honey
4. Dandelions for Dinner
5. Plum Upside Down
6. Berry on Top

Cavanagh Cowboys Romance
(Montana Ranches Christian Romance)

1. Marry Me for Real, Cowboy'
2. Give Me Another Chance, Cowboy
3. Let Me Off Easy, Cowboy

Saddle Springs Romance
(Montana Ranches Christian Romance)

1. The Cowboy's Christmas Reunion
2. The Cowboy's Mixed-Up Matchmaker
3. The Cowboy's Romantic Dreamer
4. The Cowboy's Convenient Marriage
5. The Cowboy's Belated Discovery
6. The Cowboy's Reluctant Bride

Garden Grown Romance
(Arcadia Valley Romance)

1. Sown in Love (ebook only)
2. Sprouts of Love
3. Rooted in Love
4. Harvest of Love

Riverbend Romance Novellas

1. Secretly Yours
2. Pinky Promise
3. Sweet Serenade
4. Team Bride
5. Merry Kisses

valeriecomer.com/books

CHAPTER ONE

Adam Cavanagh strode across the parking lot, his thoughts clicking right along with his boots on the slick pavement. Was he honestly slinking home like a whipped pup? He'd be right back under his stepfather's grinding thumb once he drove up the ranch road. How could that be an improvement over risking life and limb every time he blasted out of the chute on the back of a bronc?

His decision had been easy ten years ago. Get out. Make it big. Thumb his nose at Declan Cavanagh.

It wasn't so simple now. Not when Declan would throw him into the saddle with a self-satisfied grunt and order him to work like he was a delinquent child. Adam needed Door Number Three. So far, it had failed to materialize.

"Get your hands off me!" a shrill female voice demanded.

Adam tensed, his step faltering. Where was that coming from? He couldn't tell in the darkness.

A low male voice answered. The woman replied more calmly. Firmly.

She must be okay, and it probably wasn't any of his business. Plus, he was starving. Still he hesitated, scanning the parking lot again, but nothing appeared to be happening in any of the pools of light from the street lamps. Nothing besides angling sleet.

He was imagining things. It happened a lot ever since his buddy's nasty accident in the arena with thousands of fans watching. Adam shook his head and entered the Golden Grill. Man, he'd missed this place.

Please wait to be seated.

There were a few empty tables, and the aroma of fried liver and onion rings wafted his way. His stomach growled. Where was the hostess, anyway?

The door behind him swung open, ushering in the late October night. Adam glanced over, and his gaze collided with a woman with wild eyes and hair to match. She wore jeans, a down parka, and a ratty backpack over her shoulder. Cowboy boots on her feet. Good Montana girl. He nodded in approval.

She hesitated, glancing around the restaurant, back through the door closing behind her, then over at Adam.

What was with her? He couldn't help grinning. She was stinkin' cute. If that had been her yelling in the parking lot, he wouldn't mind coming to her rescue one little bit.

She launched at him, and her arms wrapped around his neck. "Pretend you love me. Kiss me."

Who was Adam to argue with an invitation like that? Besides, his arms had already shot around her, mostly to keep his balance from the impact of her compact body.

He kissed her.

She kissed him back. Wow, did she ever.

The door cranked open again. Footsteps. Boots, again. Heavier this time. "Riley! I didn't mean — whoa."

Adam caressed her lips for a few seconds longer, but he really needed to see what trouble had arrived on the heels of this thirty-second diversion.

The girl — Riley? — opened her eyes slowly and smiled up at him. "Thanks," she breathed. "You're a lifesaver."

Being her hero sounded good. He pressed his lips to her forehead and looked over her tangles to see the guy she'd been escaping from. No way.

"Scotty Erickson?" Adam couldn't keep the disbelief out of his voice. It was probably reasonable to run into people from his past when he was less than an hour from the family ranch, but why did the first guy he saw have to be this dirt-bag? He tightened his arms around Riley. If Scotty wanted a woman who didn't want him back, he'd have to go through Adam to get her.

"You." Scotty all but spat the word. "Let go of my girl. Come on, Riley. Enough stalling. Time to hit the road. Looks like it might start snowing soon."

Riley shook her head slightly against Adam's chest.

"*Your* girl?" Adam managed a sneer in his tone. "Ry, honey, you two-timing me?"

She blinked up at him, her back still to the other guy. "Never."

That sounded promising. "Get lost, Erickson."

Scotty braced his feet.

Adam took a quick scan for a weapon but didn't see one. The scum wouldn't likely be that stupid. "Hey, did you get a chance to pick up the engagement ring today?" He nuzzled Riley's hair, still eyeing Scotty. "When will they be done resizing it?"

She pulled back.

He got a little distracted by those wide eyes. Oh, and the soft lips. He kissed her again.

"Uh... not yet." She sounded breathless. "Maybe in a few days."

"The sooner the better. I can't wait to make you my own."

Scotty scoffed. "Get in line, Cavanagh."

"We don't want any trouble in here. Do I need to call the police?" A pudgy middle-aged man stood beside the hostess desk, eyebrows raised.

Adam hesitated. Erickson and the host didn't seem to know each other. He shook his head. "Not at all. My fiancée and I met here for a peaceful celebratory dinner." Adam jutted his chin toward Scotty. "He was just leaving."

The host hesitated, his gaze ricocheting between them.

Adam turned his back on Scotty and threaded his fingers with Riley's. "If you've got a booth away from the window, that would be perfect. Right, honey?"

"Sure would!" Riley glanced back at Scotty but stayed with Adam as he followed the man to a booth at the other end.

He slid in across from her. Wow, he'd lucked out this evening after all. She was cute as a filly and sassy besides. Too bad kissing was his limit these days.

"Your server will be right with you." The man set two menus at the end of the table. "Can I get you something to drink in the meanwhile?"

Was that a flash of wariness in Riley's eyes?

"Ginger ale and a black coffee, please." Part of that whole new leaf thing. Besides, he needed his wits about him. "How about you, honey?"

"Ice water." She stared at him as though calculating. "With lemon."

The host nodded and stepped away.

Adam flipped open the embossed menu, but the aroma of liver and onions still called his name. None of the other entrees looked more appealing. "What're you having? Order whatever you like."

"Why?" Her elbows plunked on the table. "Why are you buying me dinner and being so nice to me?"

He leaned against the padded seatback and set his hat beside him.. "Why not?"

"I don't even know your name. Or why Scotty seems to know you."

"The name's Adam Cavanagh."

She didn't blink.

Apparently she didn't follow the rodeo circuit. So, she wasn't *quite* perfect, after all. "My stepdad owns Rockstead Ranch northeast of town. And I may have missed your name, too. Riley...?"

"Riley Dunning." She licked her lips in a nervous gesture. "Born in Missoula and raised all over the west."

"Riley Cavanagh has a nice ring to it, don't you think?" He might have asked blandly, but his mind was skittering. Had a third option shown up, after all? There might be more than one way to shake up things at Rockstead.

"You're some kind of crazy."

Adam belted out a laugh. "You're the one who asked a complete stranger to kiss her."

ONE MINUTE RILEY was trying to ditch Scotty's slimy attention and the next she sat across from a hot cowboy in a Golden Girls themed diner with carte blanche to order what she wanted.

She'd see if he meant it. Who knew when she'd eat again?

When the server returned, Adam indicated she should order first.

Riley pointed to the menu's Friday-night special. "Steak, medium rare, and crab legs. I'll take the baked potato with extra sour cream, and may I have the Caesar instead of the house salad?" She looked up at the server, avoiding eye contact with Adam.

Here's your chance to back down, buster.

He leaned across the table and tapped the appetizer section on the facing page. "Sure you don't want a starter to kick off that feast?"

If he was going to be *that* way about it... Riley met his gaze and locked on. "Go ahead and order for both of us."

Adam nodded and looked at the server. "We'll have the nacho platter first, please. I'll take liver and onion rings for my entree. Mashed potatoes and double up the gravy. The house salad is fine for me."

"Right away, sir." The server gathered the menus and bowed away.

The cowboy narrowed his gaze at her for so long Riley squirmed. "You said I could order anything."

"I did. Meant it, too."

Whew. "Then what's the problem?"

Adam reached over the table and caught Riley's hands. "Tell me how you know Scotty." His hands were strong and rough and tanned, with a thin scar running from his wrist to his thumb.

She resisted the urge to trace it. "He seemed to think I owed him something because I hitchhiked a ride from him."

"What's a nice girl like you doing hitchhiking?'

Riley raised her chin. "Who said I was a nice girl?"

A glimmer of humor shone in his eyes. "The other kind would have considered giving Erickson what he wanted."

"He can't keep his hands to himself."

Adam tipped his head back and chuckled.

What was so hilariously funny? She glared at him before becoming aware of his fingers squeezing hers. Oh. She pulled away, and he let her, though he laughed even harder.

He was so exasperating. And, yes, she owed him. Not only for rescuing her, but for an extravagant dinner.

Exasperating, but such a hunk, even with his unruly hair creased from the Stetson he'd been wearing. His face was strong and angular with a slightly crooked nose like he'd broken it once or twice. His lips... well, she shouldn't be looking at those, because he was an amazing kisser. Like that was any test of a decent human being.

He'd rescued her, though. Kissed her like she'd

demanded. Held her tight against his broad, firm chest and sent Scotty packing.

Pretended they were engaged.

Riley shivered.

The server set their drinks and the nachos between them.

She reached for a chip and dragged it through the spicy cheese. It tasted even better than it smelled, and *that* had been amazing.

"Have you eaten today?"

Riley's gaze shot back to Adam's. "Um... not much."

"How come?"

He couldn't possibly really want to know.

She ate three more chips, but his gaze didn't waver. "It's a long story," she said at last. "I doubt you want to hear the details."

Adam's gaze only intensified. "Try me."

"I'm... let's just say I'm between situations and leave it at that." She eyed him. "Besides, I don't know anything about you."

He shrugged. "Already told you where I live. My stepdad operates two of the biggest ranches in the region. My brothers and I will be taking one of them over when the time is right." He studied her for a long moment.

"What, do I have salsa on my chin?" Riley dabbed with her napkin.

"Not at all. Just thinking... maybe the time is right."

Now he was getting weird. "Pardon me?"

"I've been away a long time. My stepdad and I don't see eye-to-eye on a lot of things, and he hasn't been willing to let me prove myself. I think he'd take me more seriously if I were engaged."

Riley stared at him. "Come again?"

"People break engagements all the time. It doesn't mean a life sentence."

"Wait a minute. You're asking me—"

His phone rang, and he held up one finger to silence her.

It annoyed her like crazy that it worked.

"Yo, Nathaniel. What's up?" Adam took a sip of his ginger ale then set the glass down with a clunk. The ice cubes rattled as his gaze shot back to Riley's. "Erickson's faster than I gave him credit for."

Uh oh. She should have paid more attention to the fact that Scotty and Adam seemed to know each other.

"Yes, that's what he heard ... I didn't tell anyone about Riley because she's a surprise."

Riley snorted.

Laugh lines crinkled around Adam's eyes as he grinned at her. "We haven't made any firm plans yet ... Definitely, bro. You'll be the first to know ... How're things at home? How's Mom?"

He had a mother? He'd talked about his stepfather as though the man were his only parent.

Jaw tensing, Adam looked down at his free hand lining up the cutlery with the edge of the table. "Sorry to hear that ... Riley and I are waiting to be served, so we'll be a couple of hours at least ... Tell Mom I'll see her in the morning then ... You too, bro. Later."

Riley crossed her arms over her chest. "What's going on?"

9

"Erickson told his sister who told my brother who told my other brother who was understandably surprised since I didn't have a girlfriend yesterday. At least that he knew of."

"Sorry?"

"Don't be."

The server chose that moment to set their entrees in front of them. "Can I get you anything else?"

"I think we're good for now." Adam spread his cloth napkin on his lap.

Riley should do the same. She stared at the heaped platter in front of her. The steak was perfectly crisscrossed, and the crab legs joined the beef in sending up a mouth-watering aroma. If she had to get a to-go container later, that would be okay. It'd give her something for breakfast. Best to start with the crab in that case.

She reached for the cracker tool then became aware Adam was still studying her. "What?"

"What are your plans for the next few weeks?"

"Um..." Her mind scrambled, trying to come up with something that sounded believable or important.

"Christmas with your family?"

Right, the holidays were coming. "I don't think so. My parents are..." *Remember how lying was a bad idea?* "Busy this year."

"How are you with horses?"

Riley blinked. "I've ridden some." Not as much as the rich kids she'd known.

"Come with me. We can always use another hand at the ranch. And I need a fiancée until about the new year. What do you say?"

Her jaw dropped as she stared at him. "What's in it for me? Besides you keep your hands to yourself." She couldn't believe for one minute she was entertaining his ridiculous offer.

Amusement glinted in his eyes. "Wouldn't it look odd if I didn't touch my future wife? Besides, she's pretty demanding about being kissed."

A flush crept up Riley's cheeks.

"There will be honest hard work you'll get paid for. A good reference at the other end." He leaned on the table, wholly focused on her. "And did I mention kissing?"

What a preposterous offer. She really ought to laugh him off.

CHAPTER TWO

Even the sudden silence from the woman across the table couldn't keep Adam from enjoying his dinner. Not every cook had mastered perfectly tender, delectable liver, but it was a Golden Grill specialty. Estelle must still be in the kitchen.

For all that Riley had ordered the biggest entree on the menu, she seemed to have lost her appetite.

Adam didn't usually have this effect on women. Well, except the ones who spent their lives calling half a cup of salad a meal so they could stay in their size zero jeans.

Riley was a healthier armful.

She caught his gaze and offered a narrowed look in return.

He grinned at her. "Well, what do you think?"

"I think you're loco. What I'm not sure of is if I should call the cops."

"I'm not that kind of crazy." He cut a breaded onion ring in half and forked a piece into his mouth.

"Normal people don't ask strangers to pretend-marry them. And they don't eat liver."

"Liver's loaded with nutrients your body needs, like Vitamin A. It's tasty besides. Want a bite?"

Riley pulled back, her lip curling. "Not a chance. It even smells gross."

"Your loss." Adam shrugged and scooped up a large dollop of mashed potatoes dripping with gravy.

"You know what they tell you in Stranger Danger 101, right? Suspect everyone."

Adam snorted a laugh. "Says the girl who hitchhiked from... where? I don't think you ever did say."

"I didn't." She focused on sprinkling bacon bits over her sour-cream-loaded baked potato.

"I told you everything there was to know about me." Okay, that wasn't totally true, but she knew where he lived, his family dynamics, and why he'd proposed. Fake proposed.

"You have two brothers?"

He chuckled. Okay, so he'd missed some details. "More like five of them. And two sisters."

Her eyes widened. "That's a huge family."

Once upon a time he'd lived with two parents who loved him and his younger brothers. It had been an idyllic life at Running Creek Ranch, even if the twins were a unit and he'd been solo. That didn't mean he'd approved of Mom marrying Declan, especially with some nonsense of it being better for her sons.

It had not been better. From the very first minute, it had been Declan's sons versus Kathryn's sons. Great way to grow up, and why he'd left Rockstead Ranch right after high school and never looked back. Until now.

He met Riley's gaze. "One of those his-and-hers-and-theirs families. Declan's wife left him with three boys. My dad passed away and my mom married Declan. So that accounts for the six boys. Then Mom and Declan had a set of twins. Girls, this time. They turned thirteen last spring."

Alexia and Emma were the only bright spot in the entire fiasco that was his mother's second marriage. But, man, they were a handful. Declan might have figured out how to keep six young bucks roughly pointed toward the straight-and-narrow, but those girls tap-danced all over him. Mom had given up, as well. Without the intervention of their big brothers, the twins would be in much worse shape.

Sore spot. Adam had been gone too much to be much help. Now that he was home, he'd make sure his sisters straightened up.

He eyed Riley. "How are you with teenage girls?" At least she'd been one once.

Riley choked on a crouton and coughed it up. She dabbed her mouth with a folded paper napkin, mumbled "excuse me" and bolted toward the restrooms, her back-pack dangling from her hand.

Adam finished his plate, but still she didn't return. Had she left the restaurant? Maybe she'd just been after a meal — not that she was anywhere near done — and decided to go back to Scotty. Maybe it had all been a setup to get free food.

Nah. He was better at reading people than that.

Wasn't he?

He stretched out in the booth with his back to the wall, settled his hat on his head, dug out his phone, and checked the news.

"Is the lady done? May I remove your plates?" The server stood at the end of the table, his face questioning.

"She'll be back, but you can take mine. Thanks."

"Dessert, sir?"

Temptation. The diner had a reputation for the best cheesecake in western Montana. "No, thank you. I'm ready for the bill. Maybe a to-go container for the lady, just in case."

"Yes, sir. Right away."

Adam would enjoy that steak for a bedtime snack if Riley had really abandoned him. Didn't women always take what they wanted and then ditch the guy? Seemed like standard behavior from where he sat.

Even Mom had done that to Declan but, in that case, the guy deserved it. Adam might've been only thirteen and wet behind the ears as far as love went, but he hadn't been able to figure out why Mom had agreed to the neighboring rancher's proposal. Still couldn't. Adam could have helped her keep the ranch running. They hadn't needed Declan.

When the server returned, Adam paid the bill with a decent tip for the scene they'd caused and began packing up Riley's leftovers.

She'd stood him up.

So much for Door Number Three. Slammed shut in his face. Too bad. She'd felt mighty nice in his arms there for a few minutes.

"WHAT DO YOU MEAN, you quit college?" Riley paced the restaurant's small restroom with her cellphone pressed to her ear. The four actresses who'd played the Golden Girls seemed to watch her every move from their posters on the walls.

"Mick is amazing. Just wait until you meet him."

Riley'd put that off as long as she could, thanks. "No guy is worth quitting school for."

Her sister sighed heavily into the phone. "I told you. We're taking turns. First I'll put Mick through college, then he'll do the same for me. It will take a bit more time, but we won't be saddled with huge loans at the other end. Win, win!"

Lose, lose.

Riley leaned her head against the door just as it opened and crashed into her. She jumped back, rubbing her forehead.

"Oh, I'm sorry." An older lady with a cane edged into the restroom past Riley. "This space is so small. I didn't mean to hurt you, dear. I just didn't see you."

"I'm fine." At least her forehead would be. Inside her brain, not so much. "Jodie, how long have you known Mick?"

The old lady closed a stall door behind her.

"Since school started in September. We're in some of the same classes."

"You mean were."

"Um. Yes."

"You can't just do this."

"I already did. Don't tell me what to do, Riley. It's not like you've got your life all together. Got a better plan?

Show me how much better you can do, and I'll consider following in your footsteps."

"I'm getting married." No sooner had the words exploded from her mouth than she wished them back. She had *not* made this decision. Not at all. Plus, it was entirely fake.

"You're *what?* I thought you broke up with Raul."

The old lady edged out of the stall and smiled at Riley as she approached the sink. "Congratulations, dear."

Riley rubbed her forehead. "Thank you."

"I didn't say anything for you to thank me for!" yelled Jodie. "You're crazy. You just hitchhiked from New Mexico, Mom and Dad don't know where you are, and now you're getting married to some guy we haven't even met? Don't go telling me how to live my life when you obviously don't have yours put together."

"So I guess couch-surfing at your place for a few days is out of the question..."

"You bet it is. Mick and I have a studio apartment. There's no room for you. Besides, you've got a fiancé. Go move in with him."

"It's not like that." Riley waited while the old lady dried her hands under the noisy blower.

"What's it like then?"

"We're not sleeping together."

The old lady smiled. "Good for you." Then she left the room.

"Oh, here we go again. 'Keep your jeans zipped, Jodie. Be a good girl, Jodie.' Well, I'm not the one who ditched her boyfriend and promptly got engaged to a guy I don't even know. Who is he? Are you pregnant? When did you meet him? Like, yesterday?"

More like an hour ago. "Never mind, sis. I'll call you for coffee next time I'm in Missoula." She'd been headed to the small Montana city, but Scotty was only going as far west as Jewel Lake. It shouldn't be hard to thumb another ride the rest of the way, but for what, when Jodie didn't want her?

Surely Adam would let her off his ranch a time or two between now and the end of her sentence. She couldn't believe she was considering his preposterous offer. That her mouth had apparently affirmed what her mind was still battling with.

Jodie huffed. "Fine. I look forward to it." The dead air that followed her sister's words belied their meaning.

Nice. Riley'd gone and burned another bridge. How many did that make in the past few days? Too many to recover from. Hiding out at Adam's ranch was sounding better and better. Men were all either slimy or demanding jerks. She'd keep her heart intact this time. She and Adam would be friends with benefits. Limited benefits. And then she'd march out with enough cash to get a new start somewhere.

First, though, she should Google the guy. She thumbed open her search app and tapped the microphone. "Adam Cavanagh."

Huh, so that's how it was spelled.

Riley Cavanagh has a nice ring to it, don't you think?

She shoved his bland words out of her mind as search results popped up. No way. The guy was some kind of rodeo celebrity. He'd just won an all-around championship down in Texas, and had been seen dating megastar Chantelle Devereaux? Whoa. No wonder he seemed so self-assured. He had it made.

Hmm. He was probably loaded.

Not that Riley was mercenary. Exactly. But he'd offered to pay her handsomely, whatever that was, for honest work. And she did need to lie low for a bit. She couldn't stay with Jodie.

It wasn't taking advantage of a guy if he made an offer and she agreed, was it? Because this beat all her other options to pieces. Basically, all he was doing was offering her a job and giving her a chance to play a role. She'd liked drama in high school.

She could pull this off and come out of it with a fresh start in front of her. Teenage girls, though. With Raul thousands of miles away, it should be okay.

Riley tightened her backpack straps, yanked open the restroom door, and marched toward the table where Adam stood, stacking several to-go containers together.

See? Nice guy. She'd still get her dinner.

He looked up at her approach, brows shooting up into the shadows of his dark cowboy hat. "And here I thought you'd abandoned me."

"We're going to talk. Outside."

Humor glinted in his gorgeous eyes. "Whatever you say, honey."

She ground her teeth as she led the way to the door. He must have already paid, since he didn't pause at the hostess desk but reached past her to push the door open. "After you."

The wind whipped icy pellets against her face. The

outside air had definitely dropped a few degrees while they'd been inside. Well, her internal temperature had gone up in the same interval. She'd survive.

Adam led the way to a big, black truck hitched to a horse trailer at the edge of the lot. A horse whinnied, and he talked soothingly to the animal. "Not long now, Jupiter. Not long." Then he opened the passenger door for Riley.

She crossed her arms and braced her feet. "How much?"

"How much what?"

"How much money you're offering."

He tipped his head back and laughed. "So we're back to that, are we?"

"Never agree to a new position without knowing what the job description and compensation are."

"Fair enough. What do you want to get out of this?"

Riley narrowed her gaze at him. "Ten grand."

"For three months of pretending to be my fiancée?"

"Yup."

"I'll throw in an engagement ring you can pawn later if you want."

Riley blinked. He'd give her ten grand *and* a ring? "Seriously?"

"Sure. No one will believe me if you aren't wearing a diamond, but it does mean we need to spend the night in town." He held up one hand. The other still held the stack of to-go containers. "I'll get you a hotel room at the Last Chance. I'll bunk in the truck near Jupiter. Won't be the first time."

Riley studied him. What was not to like? The guy was hotter than New Mexico and seemed a gentleman. "And we buy a ring in the morning?" Maybe a few clothes, too, since she wouldn't be raiding Jodie's closet, after all.

He nodded. "Then head up to Rockstead Ranch, where you become my loving girlfriend."

"But not too loving."

Adam's eyes twinkled. "Of course."

She stuck out her hand. "Deal."

CHAPTER THREE

I t wasn't until they turned north off the highway that Riley stopped staring at the large diamond on her left hand and began paying attention to the landscape.

They bumped over a cattle guard and wound between rolling hills dotted with yellowed shrubs. The gravel road curved down along a creek lined with conifers then began to climb. Taller mountains peeked from the distance several times.

Riley had forgotten how blue Montana's big sky could be after a rain. How expansive the landscape, even late in the fall when wildflowers and green grass were but a vague memory.

"This is beautiful."

Adam shot her a look across the cab, his hands flexing on the wheel. "All Rockstead land."

His stepdad's holdings. "Where's the other ranch?"

He thumbed toward the east. "Next property over."

"Maybe sometime you can show me."

"Maybe." His jaw tightened, and he slowed for another cattle guard.

Twenty minutes later he rounded two final tight curves and the truck emerged into a tree-lined valley. Whoa. That was a massive log-and-rock house on the right, tucked against a copse of trees, while a huge red barn loomed in front of them. Half a dozen horses grazed behind white rail fences, and several pickup trucks dotted the gravel parking area.

But Riley's gaze swung back to that immense, pristine house. It sure looked big enough to house a family of eight kids with room to spare. But Adam wasn't exactly a kid anymore.

He followed the gravel drive past the house and barn, past a long, low stable, and around another curve. A row of small log cabins appeared nestled against the trees. Finally, Adam pulled a tight right, then expertly backed the horse trailer to a gate.

Riley hadn't given Jupiter a second thought. She assumed Adam had cared for his horse last night and this morning, but her thoughts had been consumed by the man... and the situation she'd agreed to.

Now she hopped down from the cab and watched as Adam entered the trailer.

He spoke softly — Riley strained to hear his words — and then the huge, brown horse backed down the ramp, Adam by its head. "Here you go, Jupiter. We're back in Montana. Lots of room to run." He slid his hands over the horse's back and legs.

Jupiter leaned against Adam's shoulder, and the cowboy

wrapped his arms around the horse's neck for a long moment.

Okay, whatever Riley was getting into way out here in the middle of nowhere, Adam himself wasn't a danger to her. Not if he were this gentle with his mount.

He might be a danger to her heart, but she'd be strong. Three months, tops. Possibly even less, if his stepdad wasn't as iron-fisted as Adam feared. Then Riley would take her money and make her escape.

She straightened her shoulders and lifted her chin as he released the horse into the pasture. She could do this.

"Yo, Adam!"

Riley braced herself as another cowboy came up beside Adam. The two guys slammed fists with a force that should have broken knuckles then gave each other a brief, fierce hug.

"Nathaniel! Lookin' good, bro."

The newcomer looked Adam up and down and nodded. "Ditto." Then he turned to Riley, and a slow smile creased his face. "And you must be Riley."

She nodded then offered a warm smile and an outstretched hand.

Nathaniel elbowed Adam. "You've been holding out." Instead of shaking Riley's right hand, he grabbed her left, taking a good look at the massive diamond before letting go. He whistled. "I thought you were kidding me, Adam."

Adam slid his arm around Riley's waist and tugged her close. "Nope." He pressed a kiss into Riley's hair.

She leaned against him, watching his brother. If they couldn't fool the first one they met, their scheme was done for.

"Well, I never. Where'd you two meet? Never mind. There'll be time for that story later. More to the point, does the stepfather know?"

Adam's grip on her waist spasmed slightly. "Not yet, but I'm sure he saw us driving through. He'll be here any minute."

Nathaniel snorted. "You can bet your bottom dollar."

Sounded like Adam wasn't the only one with a healthy respect for his stepdad. Or maybe unhealthy. And Nathaniel was Adam's full brother, one of the twins, right? It was going to take some doing keeping this strange family straight.

"Where's Riley gonna stay? With you?" Nathaniel thumbed toward the row of cabins across the drive.

"You know better, Nat."

The younger guy shrugged. Perhaps his cheeks flushed just a little. Riley's certainly had.

"Is there an empty cabin right now?"

"Yeah, number three. Noah spends so much time on the road that he just bunks with me when he's at Rockstead."

Interesting. He didn't call the ranch home.

"I'll talk to Declan about that, then."

"And if he says no?"

Adam's fingers massaged Riley's side. "He won't unless he has other plans for it."

"Or other plans for you."

Riley glanced up as Adam stiffened. What would a loving fiancée say or do at that remark? She turned slightly and touched his stubbled cheek. "It'll be okay."

"Thanks for your faith in me, honey." He dropped a light kiss to her lips.

That should convince his brother and anyone else who might be watching.

"You tucked your tail between your legs and came home, huh? Rodeo's not big enough to keep you anymore?"

Riley shivered at the booming voice and allowed Adam to turn them both as a unit. She clung to his waist and took in the lean middle-aged rancher striding toward them, boots crunching on the gravel. This had to be the infamous Declan Cavanagh.

The man stopped a few feet away, piercing eyes taking them in from beneath the brim of his well-worn felt cowboy hat. His feet were braced, and his thumbs hooked through belt loops.

"Hi, Dad. Yes, I'm back."

Riley took strength from Adam's even tone.

Then Declan's gaze fixed on her. "And you are?"

She sucked in her lips to moisten them, but Adam spoke first. "This is my fiancée, Riley Dunning. I offered her a job here, and she needs a place to stay. How about cabin three? Nat says it's empty."

"What if we don't need a hand?"

This was what Riley had been afraid of. That she'd be turfed out before she even had a chance to play her part.

Adam returned his stepdad's look. "We always need a hand. She can ride or muck out stalls. Or she can help in the house or take on Alexia and Emma. You can't tell me there's nothing that needs doing."

Wait, no. He was offering her as a chaperone for two teenagers? So not happening. Except ten thousand dollars and a honkin' big diamond said she'd do it if she had to.

"You can ride?"

"Yes, sir." Riley said it as cheerfully as she could muster. Maybe her voice squeaked a little. Maybe not.

"Are you pregnant?"

Why did everyone's minds go there? She raised her chin. "I am *not*, sir."

His eyebrows rose. "You're sure?"

What, he wanted to see evidence? He could take a flying leap off the top of that ginormous red barn. Riley sent mental daggers from her eyes. "Absolutely."

"We'll talk." Declan gave Adam another probing, significant look and strode away.

Riley could feel Adam's back muscles relax slightly.

"That went pretty well," Nathaniel observed.

It had? Riley'd thought the rancher would eat her alive, but here she still was, in one piece.

Maybe it *had* gone pretty well.

ADAM DISCONNECTED the horse trailer then pulled his Dodge Ram up to the last cabin. He turned to Riley. "Home sweet home." If only he could keep the bitterness out of his voice.

"It's beautiful here, Adam." Her blue eyes shone with sincerity, and her long curly hair framed her pretty face.

"You're what's beautiful." He hadn't intended to say it, but it was true.

She snickered. "You don't need to flatter me when there's no one to overhear."

At Rockstead, there was always someone to overhear. "It's still true." He leaned across the cab and kissed her lightly. "Let me show you around. And stay put until I come open your truck door."

"Oh, the gentleman thing."

"Don't mock me, woman."

She was still laughing when he plucked her off her seat a moment later and swung her to the ground. He grabbed her hand, led her up the two steps to the covered porch, then unlocked the plank door. It had been months since he'd been home, and it showed. The air was chilly and stale.

Riley looked around, taking it all in. What did it look like to her?

"Cabin three's just like this one but mirrored. A kitchenette and front room, a full bath, and a bedroom at the back, overlooking the creek."

"Wood heat?" Her gaze fixed on the cast-iron stove.

"Yep. There's a big stack of split logs across by the machine shed." He eyed her. "Ever used a wood stove? If you'd rather not, I could probably get you a room in the house."

She shuddered. "I'll learn."

"That's my girl."

Riley rolled her eyes and peeked into the bathroom then his bedroom.

No worries. He'd left it picked up in August, last time he'd been here. There was a skim of dust on everything, but the space was small, and it wouldn't take long to freshen it up.

They'd clean hers first, if Declan allowed her a cabin. At least Cook was settled into cabin one, nearest the house, so there was a precedent for a female employee in the middle of the men's spaces.

"Let me start a fire in here, and then we'll go have a look at cabin three and get it warming, too. Then we can scrub them both." Tomorrow was soon enough to hit the saddle. Even Declan would allow that much.

Riley stood in front of his open bedroom door, head tilted to one side.

For just a second, Adam let his mind go there, but then he slammed the thoughts out. Nope. That was not how this situation was going to unfold. He wasn't living that way anymore.

Not since weeks before Ace Desjardins' accident, when Adam, Ace, and Sawyer Delgado had pledged to clean up their acts and recommit to the faith of their childhoods. Adam's had never been strong, but he remembered church with both his parents. After Dad's death and Mom's remarriage, Mom had dragged all six boys — sporting clean clothes and freshly scrubbed faces — into town on Sunday mornings and sat them in a row. It had stuck with all of them... to varying degrees.

What had happened to the strength his mother had shown back then? Oh, yeah. Declan had worn her down. The man had a lot to pay for.

"Adam?"

He blinked Riley back into focus. "Sorry. Wool-gathering."

"It's going to be okay."

Was he that obvious? Or how had a woman he'd known less than twenty-four hours read his mood so easily? "You think?"

"Sure, why not? Your stepfather is intense, but you'll win him over. You're twenty-eight, not a kid to be bossed around."

Adam narrowed his gaze. "I don't remember telling you my age."

She looked away, her face flushing.

"You ran a search, huh?" Of course she had. He'd done the same to her last night in the truck, though he'd found little.

"Yeah. Now I know all about you. I mean, what's online."

Had she gone back far enough to read the gossip rags about his relationship with the country singer last summer? She'd say something, wouldn't she? Which meant maybe she didn't know. He'd keep it that way for now. That had not been his finest moment.

He offered Riley a grin and bobbed his eyebrows. "Your Facebook is locked down to friends-only. And you haven't been in the news."

Her face blanched, and she reached for the countertop to steady herself.

Wait. What? "Anything you want to tell me, honey? Wanted in fourteen states for a crime you didn't commit?"

"Of course not." Her gaze ricocheted around the space, not meeting his, and landed on his trophy case. "Those all yours?" She crossed the room and touched one of the cast bronze statues.

"Yeah." Maybe he could forget all about the new one buried beneath everything in the truck's backseat.

She looked over. "You won another one, didn't you?"

Adam crossed his arms. "I might not put it up." Might use it for target practice.

"Why would that be?"

Her Google skills needed some work if she had no clue. "Ace Desjardins should have won it."

Riley searched his face. "But *you* did. Right?"

Only because he'd ridden before Ace, and everyone who competed afterward was too rattled to ride well. "Long story."

"Try me."

Adam swallowed hard. Did he want to talk about the freak accident that had sent one of his best buds into a coma he was still drifting in weeks later? Did he want to talk about the wallop of Ace's skull on the bronc's rear, the slo-mo tumble, the crack as the sharp hooves rammed downward? The stillness of his friend's body?

He shoved the entire memory into a box at the back of his brain and slammed the lid shut before meeting Riley's gaze.

"No." Not now. Not ever.

CHAPTER FOUR

Riley worked alongside Adam for a couple of hours, wiping down all the surfaces in both cabins and learning how to feed the fires inside the small wood stoves. It hadn't taken long for warmth to permeate the spaces, pushing out the chill.

She had to hand it to Adam. No hints that he thought cleaning was beneath him. Or maybe he was only sticking with her to protect her from unwanted visitors. She shuddered at the thought of Declan deciding to drop by and interrogate her further. Even worse, he likely had a master key to all the cabins besides the one Nathaniel had dropped by.

An online search would show her other ways to keep him out. Not that he was likely that kind of man, but a woman couldn't be too careful.

Riley turned to Adam. "What's the Wi-Fi password?"

He blinked. "The what?"

"Wi-Fi." She held up her phone. "You know... how do I get on the internet?"

"Well, two things." He dropped his rag into the bucket and looked at her, humor glinting in his eyes. "First, there aren't any other houses for nearly thirty miles, so there's no one to steal the signal."

Oh. She hadn't thought of that.

"Second, there isn't any Wi-Fi, but you can use the computer in the office at the house when you need to. It's hooked up to a satellite dish."

Riley opened her mouth in protest but closed it. Repeated the movement. "How can you live like that?" she got out at last.

Adam chuckled. "We're in the saddle from dawn til dusk around here, Ry. No one's got time to worry about the world outside."

"But..."

He shrugged. "You get used to it. I'll show you the office, and you can send an email to your friends and family to let them know you won't be phoning or texting. Or updating your Facebook."

Riley flicked on her phone. No bars. No Wi-Fi icon. No service. Great. She shoved it in her hip pocket and glared at Adam. "This might have been a deal breaker."

"You're an addict? Welcome to Rockstead Ranch, where we run IA meetings — that's internet anonymous to the uninitiated — every evening, complete with hot chocolate and s'mores around the fireplace."

Was he making fun of her? She stared at him, and he stared blandly back. "For real?" she asked finally.

"No." Voice flat, Adam turned away. "Declan would never stand for it."

"What if I don't want anyone looking at my internet

search?" Because *how to keep creepers out of my house* would only give Declan Cavanagh ideas.

Adam laughed, but it didn't sound genuine. "What are you looking up? How to hide a dead body?"

"Maybe."

He jerked to stare at her.

"Gotcha."

"You're not funny, woman."

"Lack of internet isn't funny, either, *cowboy*."

"Sorry. Never thought to mention it." He glanced at his watch. "Almost supper time, and you get to meet everyone else and see the office. And we'll grab some bedding from the house. Anything else you need?"

Riley raised her eyebrows. Like he didn't know everything she owned was in her backpack and the two shopping bags from their trip through downtown Jewel Lake this morning. At least she had a few changes of clothing and a toothbrush. Precious little for three months, but who was there to care if she wore the same outfits twice a week? Only her fiancé, and he wasn't real.

When she got off this ranch, she'd hit the mall in Missoula and buy as many jeans and shirts and cute boots as she wanted. Ten grand would go a long way.

A piercing airhorn sounded, and Riley jumped. "Oh, that scared the living daylights out of me."

"Mealtimes are announced at seven a.m., high noon, and five p.m. You'll get used to it."

She let out a long shuddering breath, nerves suddenly swamping her innards. "If you say so."

Adam stepped closer and rested both hands on her

shoulders. "You'll do fine, Ry. I'll take care of you. I promise."

If only she could believe that was totally true. She'd been looking for a man like that her entire life. But no, this was only a production fit for Hollywood, and she had a starring role. Adam, too, was only playing his part.

His lips on hers sent a different message.

Both hands on his chest, Riley shoved him away.

He narrowed his gaze as he stepped back. "What was that for?"

"Keep it to yourself when no one else is around."

"As you wish." His brown eyes darkened, and he pivoted on his heel. "Come along then. Dinner time." He held the cabin door open for her and glanced her way as they fell into step together. "May I hold your hand, your royal highness?"

She grabbed his hand. "Don't be that way."

"Don't be what way?" Adam's voice was low, intense. "Send hot and cold messages? That's you, Riley, not me. It may seem like this ranch is all wide open spaces, but it's not, at least not here at the heart of it."

How like a guy. As though she'd give him free rein to kiss her anytime he felt like it even in her cabin, just in case there was a peeping Tom? Not likely.

At first, she'd thought it was all a joke to him. Then only a ploy to get his stepdad's approval. Now it seemed he'd lured her way up in the hills to enjoy his new acting career to the hilt.

Riley stopped in the middle of the gravel drive in front of the first cabin and reached for Adam's other hand. "Listen." She kept her voice cool and low as she faced him. "We need to get through this without emotional involvement, okay? So, there are boundaries. I'm not going to change myself to be what you want. I'll do my part, but that's it. It's all business. Got it, cowboy?"

Adam's jaw clenched as he searched her eyes. "Got it." Then he leaned those extra few inches and swept his lips over hers. "Blake's watching from the barn." And he kissed her again, more thoroughly this time.

The man had far too much experience making a woman's knees turn to jelly. And he had a lot at stake.

Well, so did she. Ten grand.

She kissed him back.

"It's wonderful to meet you at last. I've heard so much about you all."

Was Riley seriously gushing at Travis? Adam should have given her the lowdown on how Declan's oldest son had hated his guts since they were kids.

Travis gave Adam a searching look before turning back to Riley. "I wish I could say the same about you, but it seems Adam's been keeping secrets."

Riley giggled. "You know how he is."

Oh, that giggle might be a little much.

"Yeah, I do. I hope you know what you're getting in for."

Riley twined her fingers with Adam's and beamed up at him. "Oh, I do. Trust me."

Batting eyelashes now? Adam nuzzled her ear. "Easy," he whispered.

"I love you, too," she whispered back, a little louder.

Oh, man. Adam was done for.

"*You're* Riley?"

Great. His thirteen-year-old sister was going for disdain. Adam turned Riley toward the twins.

Arms akimbo, Alexia looked Riley over while Emma hung back.

"Ry, honey, the one with her hands on her hips is Alexia. And the other is Emma. It's pretty easy to tell them apart. Emma's more agreeable."

Alexia's eyes flashed.

Maybe he shouldn't have goaded her.

"She looks like an improvement over your last girl-friend," Alexia announced.

Riley glanced up at him, and Adam tightened his grip on her fingers as he locked gazes with his little sister. *Not now. Not now.*

"Yeah, she was kind of..." Alexia drew a large bosom in the air in front of herself. "But she had better makeup. Fluffier hair." She demonstrated that, as well.

"A little too much, if you ask me," put in Emma. "Adam needs a real girlfriend not a megastar."

Cook saved Adam from having to answer that by calling everyone into the dining room.

Riley dragged Adam out of the family's current as they flowed into the other room. "Got something you forgot to tell me, cowboy?"

"Uh... I forgot the twins had met her." He rubbed the back of his neck. "She's been out of the picture for months. No love lost."

"She'd better be good and gone, because if I have to act like a jealous girlfriend, I can do that. Try me."

Oh... temptation. He could just see Riley going toe-to-toe with Chantelle Devereaux. His money would be on Riley Dunning, every single time.

Adam grinned at her. "You're awesome, you know that? And now we'd better get to the table, or Cook won't let us eat."

"You better tell me that story, cowboy."

"Later. With hot chocolate and s'mores." And he escorted his fiancée into the dining room to meet the rest of the family. All things considered, she was doing pretty well.

RILEY THOUGHT she had them all straight. Declan sat at the head of the table, and Cook served him first. Then Travis, Blake, and Ryder across the table. Those were Declan's sons, with Nathaniel beside them. On this side, the twins then her and Adam. Noah, the sixth brother, wasn't home, and the place at the foot of the table was set but vacant. Adam's mother had sent her apologies for a headache.

There was little small talk around the table. The twins whispered between themselves, silenced only at their father's glower. Adam's brothers reported what they'd accomplished today. Declan thought they should have achieved more and laid out his expectations for the next day, including Adam in his assignments.

What about her? The man was just intimidating enough she didn't want to draw his attention by asking what her role would be. With a giggling pair of young teens beside her, Riley was afraid their father would come to the natural conclusion of appointing her to them. If that happened, she'd need to tape a picture of ten grand to her eyelids to keep going.

Just when she couldn't take it anymore and was ready to blurt out her question, Adam's hand covered hers on her knee, squeezing lightly.

How could he peg her already? They hadn't known each other quite twenty-four hours, but here she was, in his family home, reading his cues as he read hers.

This was the kind of guy she'd like to have met when she wasn't on the run. When he wasn't conniving his way into his stepdad's good graces. When he was genuinely looking for a girlfriend... but if Chantelle Devereaux was what he went for when he wasn't up against the wall, he'd never give the real Riley a second look. After all, she was the one who'd literally thrown herself at him.

He thought she was an easy mark, and she'd done little to change that impression.

Yeah, well, she deserved to know what she was up against with previous flames. Sounded like he had a bit of a reputation from her search last night and from his siblings' comments. That shouldn't be too surprising. He was a hot-looking, self-assured cowboy with a full trophy case and a new award to add, even if he didn't want to talk about it. He must be loaded in his own right to strike a deal with her as he had.

A man like Adam would have dozens of women falling into his arms and, probably, into his bed. Not that he'd said a single inappropriate thing to Riley since they met. No hints of sharing a hotel room last night, even.

All that told her was she wasn't attractive to him. She

wasn't in his league. Somehow, she'd shown up when he needed a fake fiancée. He'd decided she could fulfill that role for a time, but she wasn't the kind of woman he could actually fall for.

He wasn't her ideal man, either, so they were even.

But as his palm warmed her knee, she found herself turning her hand over and twining her fingers with his.

He wanted her to pretend to be in love? She could do that. She could pretend the entire setup was real. It wouldn't take nearly as much acting as she'd thought last night.

Riley would have the rest of her life to recover from this fake fling. But she may as well enjoy it while she could.

CHAPTER FIVE

W hen the meal came to a close and the men had thanked the cook, Adam's brothers began excusing themselves.

Now what? Riley waited with Adam until his stepfather had left the room. Adam gave a long exhale then turned to her. "Ready to meet my mom?"

Not really. After the tension around the dinner table, Riley mostly wanted to run for the hills. Was putting up with this family worth ten grand? She studied Adam's face. Gone was the cocksure cowboy. This guy was hesitant, vulnerable.

Why was she such a sucker for a guy in need? Visions of Raul's puppy-dog eyes danced in her periphery. But Adam was different. He might be using her, but they'd spelled out the parameters. Riley was under no delusions any of this was real, but she was here until the new year sometime with a role to play.

She offered Adam a sweet smile. "Sure, why not?"

To her surprise, he led her down the staircase to the

lower level. Ahead and to the left, through an expansive family room, she made out a rounded wall of dark windows with French doors beside them. This was a walkout basement, then.

But that's not where Adam guided her. Instead he turned the other way and tapped on a door. "Mom? It's me, Adam. I've brought someone to meet you."

"Come in." The voice from inside was barely audible, but Adam pushed the door open.

The room was lit by two floor lamps. Draperies covered the far wall. There were probably windows and perhaps a door behind them, but it was solid dark outside, so the cocooning made sense. The walls were gray with several watercolor paintings. A woman sat in a gray tweed easy chair with a white afghan over her lap. There was plenty of empty space around it, a low sofa, a bookcase, and a narrow dining table with several upholstered chairs.

A Yorkie bounded across the room, yipping away.

Adam bent and scratched its scruffy head. "Hi, Ezra. Just me." Then he faced his mother and took a deep breath. "Hi, Mom. I'd like you to meet my fiancée, Riley."

The woman seated in the easy chair studied Riley.

Riley returned the favor. The woman's graying blond hair was pulled into a loose bun, and her face seemed sad.

Adam squeezed Riley's fingers. "Honey, this is my mom, Kathryn."

The woman showed no signs of rising, so Riley tugged her hand out of Adam's, crossed the space, and knelt by the chair. "I'm so pleased to meet you."

"And I, you." Kathryn patted Riley's arm before looking up at Adam. "You've been keeping secrets, son."

Adam chuckled and drew Riley to sitting on the modern sofa nearby. "I guess I have been."

Riley leaned back. He could take it from here.

"It may seem kind of sudden, but I fell for Riley the minute I met her. It's like we fell for each other at just the right instant in our lives. Right, honey?"

She batted her eyelashes up at him. "For sure." And he hadn't fallen, no matter how hard she'd run into him.

"When was that?" Kathryn's dog curled up in her lap, and she stroked his messy hair.

Adam hesitated. "A few months ago, when the rodeo was in New Mexico."

They'd beefed up their story on the drive up to the ranch and found a time and place where they could have connected. He'd told Riley how much he hated lying, but all this had been his idea, not hers. Everything after Scotty had stomped out of the Golden Grill was on him. She'd just agreed because of the money he dangled in front of her... and the fresh start he offered. And, okay, hiding out for a few months.

"How have you been doing, Mom? Did Cook bring down a plate for you?"

Kathryn's face clouded. "I wasn't hungry." By her thin frame, lack of appetite was a common occurrence.

"I'm sorry to hear you had a bad headache," Riley commented. "Was it a migraine?"

The other woman rubbed her forehead with her fingertips. "No. Just a tight band around my head."

A tension headache, then. Adam had said his mom and stepdad's marriage wasn't that great. Riley glanced surreptitiously around and noticed a door ajar to a bedroom with dusty pink bedding. Yeah, there was no way Declan would be at home down here. Suddenly, the basement made sense. She'd bet her bottom dollar he'd kept the master suite on the main level when they'd decided to give each other space. Someone had done a fine job decorating this suite, though.

Wait. Was Kathryn a prisoner? No. Couldn't be. Riley had just read *Jane Eyre* too recently. If Declan was trying to hide Kathryn, he'd no doubt do a much better job.

"We're planning a spring wedding."

Riley jerked against Adam's arm, but his fingers squeezed hers.

"Maybe we could have it in your garden?"

What garden? Riley'd thought they'd discussed the details. She'd been wrong.

"I'd like my boys to be married in the church."

"It will just be a small wedding. I... *we* thought the garden would be perfect."

We hadn't discussed a thing, but it was Riley's job to smile and nod. The wedding would never happen, anyway, so he could just go ahead and have his fun planning a phantom event.

"You told me a few weeks ago that you'd come back to your faith." Kathryn looked between them. "How about you, Riley? Are you a believer?"

"I..." Riley opened her mouth and closed it again. So much for thinking Kathryn didn't have a backbone. "Yes." Riley just hadn't given it enough thought lately, or she'd never have become embroiled with Raul.

"I'm glad to hear that. When did you make that decision?"

She'd squirm if that wouldn't give away her discomfort. Even the dog was looking at her. "When I was a child. A neighbor took my sister and me to Sunday school every week, and we went to youth group as teens later."

"Thank the Lord for godly neighbors who cared about you."

Riley'd always thought her parents had encouraged it just to have Jodie and her out of the house for a few hours, but maybe it had been God's hand. If so, she could sure use that intervention again.

Although, maybe God didn't have any use for liars. She and Adam might say they were Christians, but didn't that mean they shouldn't be pretending to be in love and engaged?

RELIEF SWEPT Adam at Riley's basic confession of faith. That was definitely a question he should have asked her before — but why? The engagement was as fake as fake could be. He'd be sure to marry a believer when the time came, but that's not what his deal with Riley was all about. This was a temporary business situation. In a few months, they'd have a public fight and break up. Then they'd shake hands in private, he'd slip her a check, and she'd be on her way. He'd miss her for a while the way a guy missed a good buddy. Nothing romantic involved.

He leaned forward. "Have you seen the doctor about your headaches, Mom?" Anything to keep the conversation focused elsewhere.

Mom closed her eyes for a brief moment. "No. They're nothing painkillers can't deal with."

"But they come often."

She chuckled softly, but her face was lined. "They do, but I can't do anything to prevent them."

"They're because of Declan."

Mom's gaze sharpened on Adam's face. "Speak respectfully."

"Why should I? He doesn't treat *you* that way."

Riley's fingers tightened in his, and Adam drew strength from her support.

"Son..."

"I'm going to ask him for the deed for Running Creek. I can't stay living here when Riley and I are married. That would be no way to start our life together, under his thumb."

She swallowed hard and looked down at Ezra for a moment. "It's a beautiful place."

Hopefully she was seeing happier memories in her mind's eye. "Maybe you'd like to move down there with us." He held his breath, searching her face.

"Oh, no. I couldn't do that. Declan—"

"Mom. It's not like you have a real marriage." It was realer than anything he and Riley would have. Apparently there were assorted levels of phoniness. Who knew?

She shook her head. "I couldn't."

"We'd love to have you," Riley offered softly.

Adam realized his thumb was stroking the back of her hand. She was crazy comforting. *All a show, dude. Remember that.*

"No..."

But his mother didn't sound as convinced as a moment ago. "Maybe a full separation would remind Declan what he had within his grasp. He's been too driven to see, and why should he change when his life is just fine? He got what he wanted when he married you — a second ranch, and someone to babysit his kids."

"Adam, don't." Mom cradled her face between both hands now.

He gentled his tone. "You know it's true. Please at least consider coming back to Running Creek with me and Riley. You and the girls. You can't deny they're just running wild here. Declan doesn't even try to control them." And didn't make it easy for Mom to do so, either. But was she even up to it? She'd run herd on three boys by herself for a year. Right, and she'd decided the job was too great for a woman alone.

How much harder could two girls be? Adam had no idea. His life had been pumped full of testosterone, and he'd left Rockstead when his sisters were mere toddlers. He was pretty sure having the twins in the house would be a lot different than a doting girlfriend, which was all the experience he'd had. Still, he needed to try.

"I couldn't take them from their father."

She meant Declan wouldn't allow it. And that might be true, but Adam was ready to go toe-to-toe with his stepfather. He needed to plan his course carefully, though. One step at a time. The right steps in the right order.

He nodded. "Promise me you'll think about it."

Mom shook her head.

But Adam knew he'd planted the seed. It would take root and grow a little before she decided either to nurture it or rip it out once and for all. "You look tired. I should let you get some sleep, and we can talk more another time." Adam rose, pulling Riley up with him. "I need to get Ry settled in cabin three. We've had a long day, too."

Mom looked between them. "Cabin three?"

"Oh, did I forget to tell you? She's staying here for a while, so giving her her own space only makes sense."

"What's your job, Riley?"

Adam forced himself not to answer for her.

"I haven't been assigned duties yet."

Because Declan was going to pretend she didn't exist for a few days before finding something conveniently unpleasant for her to do.

"And you, Adam?"

"Riding out in the morning with the guys, checking on the cattle in the east range. Should be back by the dinner bell."

Mom focused back on Riley. "Maybe you can spend the day with me."

"Um, that would be nice." Riley's words sounded cheery, but the way she clutched his hand said otherwise.

"You sure, honey?" Adam bumped her shoulder. "Don't forget you've got that big project you needed to work on."

Riley was pretty good at thinking on her feet. So far, she'd matched him toss for toss. She glanced up at him. "Oh, that. You're right." Then she turned to Mom. "I can spare a couple of hours, though. Would you prefer me to come in the morning or the afternoon?"

Good girl.

Mom sighed. "Morning. Perhaps around nine or so, while the girls are doing their schoolwork."

"I'll be here."

"Goodnight, Mom." Adam bent and kissed her cheek. "See you soon."

"It's good to have you home, my son."

Home. Rockstead had never been home to him. Never would be, either, but he wouldn't argue with her now.

Riley fluttered her fingers. "Goodnight, Kathryn."

Mom smiled. "It was nice to meet you. We'll be good friends, you and me."

Oh boy. An attachment like that wasn't something Adam had expected from his impromptu, temporary engagement. But what was not to love about Riley? Of course, his mom would be taken in. For Adam's sake... and because Riley was just that awesome.

He guided her out of his mom's suite. Thankfully, it looked quite different from when he and Travis had shared the space as teens. The basement had been enough removed from the rest of the family that no one really knew how much they'd fought. Although someone had painted over the boot marks where they'd kicked and wrestled, to say nothing of patching the holes in the drywall from ducked punches. There'd been no love lost between them. Still wasn't.

At least Travis had been civil to Riley before dinner. Maybe a messed-up girlfriend and a son he only saw on weekends was making Travis realize he wasn't the center of the universe. Never had been. Never would be.

Maybe the guy was growing up. It would be about time.

CHAPTER SIX

The house was silent when Riley ducked through the foyer and down the staircase the next morning. She took a deep breath and tapped on Kathryn's door, hoping her acting skills were up to a couple of hours with Adam's mother.

"Come in."

But that hadn't been Kathryn's voice. Riley swung open the door to find the twins sitting across from each other at the table, textbooks and notebooks spread across it.

Kathryn sat in her big chair where she'd been last night, the dog still in her lap. If she hadn't been wearing different clothes, Riley would've thought the older woman had spent the night right there.

"Saved by the girlfriend," muttered one of the twins.

What had Adam said? You could tell them apart because Emma was agreeable. So, this must have been Alexia. They weren't actually identical, though. Riley looked between them a few times, memorizing their features. "Good morning, Alexia. Hi, Emma." She only hoped she'd gotten it right.

The girls narrowed their gazes at each other, and both turned to her. "How did you know?" asked Emma.

Alexia rolled her eyes. "Lucky guess."

Let them think what they wanted. Riley didn't really want anything to do with two thirteen-year-olds, but at least their mother wouldn't likely get too personal with her daughters present.

Riley turned to Kathryn. "Good morning. I hope your headache is gone today."

"It is. Thank you."

"Mom, do we have to..."

"Alexia, finish your math."

"But—"

Her sister kicked her under the table.

"Come, sit down, Riley." Kathryn indicated the sofa. "Do you have siblings? There's nothing like twins for getting on each other's nerves."

Ah, so the kick may not have gone unnoticed. Interesting. Riley took the seat, but it was hard to get comfortable without Adam to lean against. "My sister, Jodie, is only fifteen months younger than me. We were a grade apart in school, but I'm willing to bet we had a lot of the same rivalries twins have."

Emma's eyebrows quirked.

"Did she steal your boyfriends?" Alexia asked.

"Yeah, but not when we were thirteen." Not much older, though. Jodie had always been after the boys. Good thing she hadn't laid eyes on Adam, or Mick would be gone in a flash while Jodie chased the rodeo star. No matter how hot

Mick might be, Adam would have the guy beat, hands down.

Even Raul paled in comparison. He'd swept Riley off her feet with his dark Mexican-influenced looks, so sweet and charming at first. Yeah, until she'd figured out why.

At least, with Adam, she knew the reasons. He had clear goals. This time, she knew her purpose. No pretense. Well, except toward the rest of the world. With Raul, she'd been the last to know of his manipulations.

It hadn't even taken Jodie to wreck everything. Riley's too-trusting nature had taken care of that.

Alexia tapped her pencil on the table, drawing Riley's attention. The teen eyed her blandly. "What's your favorite kind of music?"

"Uh..." Was it okay in this house not to care for country and western?

Emma glowered at her twin.

Riley's mind raced. What was this all about?

"Adam's last girlfriend was a famous pop star."

"I hope he likes pop music, then." Riley restrained herself from smacking her hand over her mouth. If she'd known Adam for months, she should know his preferences. "I meant, it's a good thing he likes it." Did he? His sisters probably knew the answer.

"She sang the national anthem at a big rodeo and thought Adam was pretty hot."

"Alexia."

The teen rolled her eyes. "What, Mother?"

If Kathryn caught the slightly snarky tone of voice, she ignored it. "We don't talk that way."

"*You* might not," the girl muttered.

"Have you ever listened to Chantelle Devereaux's music?" Emma leaned both elbows on the table as she studied Riley.

"Some, yes. She's got that new song, *If I Only Knew*, that's really awesome." It had been released as a single just a few weeks ago... suddenly Riley's brain caught up.

Alexia crossed her arms. "That song is about Adam."

"Alexia."

The girl raised her eyebrows at her mother. "Have you even listened to it? All that stuff about the cowboy who got away and how disillusioned she was to discover she'd been deceived? There's nothing else she could have been referring to."

The lyrics jostled through Riley's brain, each successive stanza elbowing the others out of the way. Maybe Alexia was right. The song reeked of Adam.

Riley forced a laugh. "Oh, that's one way to look at it, I guess. Her loss is my gain." She'd keep the lyrics in mind for her personal theme song after she and Adam split up. Who knew she'd have something in common with someone so famous? A broken heart, courtesy of Adam Cavanagh.

Broken heart? Nah. She knew better. The guy might be a total charmer, but she knew where she stood from the start. No time to wallow in that right now.

Not when she had to keep her wits about her to keep their ruse up in front of Adam's mother and sisters.

ADAM EDGED Jupiter closer to Nathaniel as they moved a herd of cattle to the east range. The grass was dry on the stalk there, thinner than over the summer, but plenty of grazing remained until the snow came. The western flanks of the Continental Divide south of Glacier Park got more rain than much of the rest of Montana. Certainly more than central Texas.

He might not think of Rockstead as home, but the rangeland? Definitely. A guy could sit atop his horse and breathe in the clean mountain air. Could see the vistas and the conifers and maybe a glimpse of some wildlife. Next year he'd be here for hunting season. He'd bring home an elk for the freezer to Riley — no, she'd be gone by then.

What good was Running Creek's old-fashioned farmhouse without a woman in it?

Nathaniel drew up Kingpin beside him. "And now you see why I never wanted to leave."

"It's gorgeous every time of year."

"Yep. Never figured why you didn't want to be here. I see the love of the land all over your face."

"It's Declan's."

Nathaniel shrugged.

Why didn't his brother understand? "I want Running Creek back. Then I'll stay." Adam shot a sidelong look at Nat. "Join me?"

"Sounds good. It's still in Mom's name, right?"

Adam shook his head. "She signed it over to Declan when they got married."

"You're kidding, right?"

"Wish I were, bro, but no. It was part of their deal, along

with him adopting us boys. I don't know what Mom was thinking."

"I didn't think to ask."

Nathaniel had never seemed to have the same drive his brothers did. Adam had never been able to figure out why. Even Noah had apprenticed as a blacksmith then bought out his mentor when the older man retired. He might keep his home base at Rockstead, but he shod horses on a circuit through western Montana, even around Saddle Springs where some of Adam's friends lived.

"Well, I asked." Declan had cuffed him on the head for being a cheeky upstart. Adam had left for the rodeo circuit a week later. "I'll get it now, though, one way or another."

The cattle milled at the narrow entrance to the valley below them, stalling, and Adam nudged Jupiter into action, circling to the north while Nathaniel headed south. Together they encouraged the cows to keep moving through the gap.

No shock when Travis angled his mount toward him.

The moment had been building all day, with Travis shooting glowering looks whenever they neared each other. Thankfully, his stepbrother hadn't let his antagonism keep him from focusing on the day's task, but now that they were on the homestretch, Adam's luck had run out.

Travis reined in beside Adam and set his cowboy hat more firmly on his head. "What're you doing back here?"

"Now there's a warm welcome if I ever heard one."

Travis snorted. "No need to pretend. We know where we stand with each other."

Yep, they did. Travis was Declan's eldest, and he'd hated

giving up the top spot to Adam when their parents married. Adam had never been able to convince the younger guy he wasn't after anything. If Travis wanted his dad's attention, he was welcome to it, but of course Declan never gave approval to any of the boys. Travis had decided it was Adam's fault.

Adam knew better. Six sons were only a workforce to Declan Cavanagh. Strapping boys he could bend to his will and turn into likenesses of himself. The man's firstborn was practically his clone, getting his way by asserting himself over the others.

"Well? Scotty sounded mighty surprised to hear of your engagement."

Adam sucked in a long breath. "Since when do you care about anything Erickson says? The guy lies through his teeth more than he tells the truth."

"Why would he lie about this? He said he gave Riley a ride clear from south of Casper, and she never said a thing about meeting up with you."

"So?" Adam tilted his hat back and stared his stepbrother down. "Why would you take his word for anything?"

"Watch how you talk about Dakota's brother."

"Oh, you two are on again?" Adam couldn't keep track. Dakota had given birth to Travis's son — what was it, three years ago or so? — but they'd broken up a few months later. Between sharing custody of Toby, both of them dated other people. And by dated, Adam wouldn't be surprised if another woman showed up claiming her kid was Travis's.

He was pretty sure no woman could make a similar claim on him, but he wasn't absolutely certain. After all, two of his rodeo buddies had recently been blindsided by the discovery of impending fatherhood.

Ace Desjardins would likely never meet his child. The former bronc rider had been in a coma since a few hours after Vanessa had dropped her verbal bomb on him. She'd rattled his focus, all but causing his freak accident in the arena, and now she was playing the grieving pregnant girlfriend.

And Sawyer Delgado's summer affair had also resulted in a pregnancy. The cowboy was currently embroiled in a fight to keep his fling from giving the baby up for adoption.

"Is she pregnant?"

Adam blinked at Travis. Why did everyone go there? Even he had. "No. We haven't slept together."

"Oh, goody-boy. How nice and honorable of you."

"Look, what's your problem?" His composure was just about shot. "What's it to you, anyway? You live your life, and I'll live mine."

"You're back at Rockstead, and that makes you my business."

"I told you when we were kids I don't care about this ranch. As far as I'm concerned, it's all yours."

"Then why are you here?"

"Because my mother lives here. My two brothers live here." He leaned a little closer to Travis, their stirrups nearly touching. "And my two sisters live here."

"Don't even mess with their minds."

"What, now they're your property, too? Don't think so, Trav. They're my sisters just as much as they're yours."

"They sure don't need you filling their heads with all your weird ideas."

"My weird ideas? If you're talking about me *not* sleeping with my fiancée, I gotta wonder how you'd feel if Alexia or Emma got pregnant anytime soon. There's something to be said for not hopping in and out of the sack all the time."

Travis's face darkened. "Don't start with me."

"You're the one who initiated this conversation, bro."

"I'm not your bro."

"You got that right. I'm also no threat to your little empire, so save your bluster for where it matters. Spend your time patching things up with Dakota. Do better than your father."

"You don't know what you're talking about."

"That's quite possible." Adam shrugged. "How about we get the rest of these cows through the draw and into the valley? That's all that's on today's agenda." Much as he'd like to add punching his stepbrother to it.

CHAPTER SEVEN

You said you can ride." Adam snapped a piece of straw and stuck it between his teeth as he gave Riley a sidelong look. "Time to prove it."

Riley took a long, deep breath. "It's been a long time."

"It's like riding a bike."

In his dreams. "I doubt that."

She'd been leaning on the corral fence, watching the horses graze the yellowing grass in the near pasture, when he'd appeared beside her, interrupting her thinking time. She hadn't been pondering riding, that was for sure.

Adam leaned a little closer, pressing his arm against hers. Warmth shot from the contact all the way through her. *Down, girl. He's not really yours.*

"Better now than when my stepfather decides to test your mettle."

"I shouldn't have told him I could ride."

"You told me first."

"Oh. Yeah. I guess I did."

He studied her from mere inches away. "So tell me about your riding experience. Time to come clean, honey."

"Stop with the honey. There's no one to hear."

"Don't count on it. Even the horses have ears."

She could argue this, but he'd win. He always did, but hearing the endearments from his lips — to say nothing of the kisses from the same location — were messing with her brain.

Riley angled a look westward where the sun already hovered over the gap in the rolling autumn hills. "It's too late in the day."

"Nice try, Ry. Then you won't have to ride for as long. Odds are, you'll be able to walk again tomorrow. Bonus, right?"

Ugh. She'd forgotten how sore she'd be. "I don't want to."

"Riley." His tone held a note of warning.

She sighed, set her hands on the top rail, and leaned back. "Fine. Whatever."

"That's better." He poked his chin toward the horses. "Which one do you want to try?"

"Um, I get a choice? I pick some old nag who's safe with five-year-olds."

He chuckled. "I don't think we have anything like that besides my nephew's pony, and you're a little taller than Toby."

"Toby?"

"Travis's kid. He's three. You'll meet him Friday when Dakota drops him off for the weekend." Adam raised his eyebrows at her. "Dakota is Scotty Erickson's sister."

"Oh." Clickety-click, the pieces snapped together. "They share custody?"

"Yep. They also share an on-again, off-again relationship." Adam stared across the pasture, his jaw pulsing.

Whoa. Somebody felt strongly. "You got a thing for her?"

"What?" Adam straightened and pinned her with all the force of his gaze. "Are you kidding me?"

"Just wondered."

"Well, don't." He grabbed her shoulders and kissed her with a boatload of passion.

One of his brothers must be nearby. She fisted the front of Adam's denim jacket in both hands and kissed him back. When they came up for air, she whispered, "Who's watching?"

He looked her in the eyes. "No one."

"Then..."

"Don't mess with me, Riley. This isn't a joke to me. When I tell you there's nothing, I mean that there is *nothing*. Got it?"

"Okay. Fine." She edged backward, trying to break his magnetic gaze. At least he released her arms. "Your sisters told me about Chantelle Devereaux." She wouldn't have thought his gaze could sharpen any further. It could.

"Don't believe everything they say. Chantelle was a mistake."

"Maybe I'm another one." From bruised lips to a bruised ego, this was going to be a difficult few months. And that wasn't even counting the bruised backside she was going to get from unaccustomed riding.

Adam offered a grunt and shook his head. Disgusted with her, most likely. "I'm going to put you on Ladybug."

"Was that the horse Chantelle rode?"

Oy. Now she'd done it. Her skull nearly split from the piercing gaze.

"I never brought Chantelle to Rockstead. In fact, I've never brought a girl here in my life before yesterday."

"You keep the real girlfriends away and just bring the fake one? I get it."

"You don't get anything, woman. Now stop talking like that. Want to accuse me of things and yell at me? Have the decency to wait until we're twenty minutes down the trail. I'm saddling Ladybug for you, unless you want to do it yourself?" One eyebrow arched.

"Please saddle her for me, cowboy." She couldn't quite keep the edge out of her own voice. God knew she'd tried.

"I'll teach you how next time." Adam stabbed a finger toward the ground between them. "You wait right here."

"Could you quit ordering me around like I'm a kid?"

"Could you not push all my buttons?"

"Like you're not pushing mine."

Adam inhaled and shook his head. "I'll be right back."

Don't make Adam angry. Wowza. She'd remember that. But how in the world could she compete with a household-name pop star? She, Riley Dunning, with zero talents, zero money, and zero charm?

She wasn't supposed to. She was supposed to practice her one talent, acting. Everyone around them was to believe she was madly in love with Adam. Of course, couples argued all the time. As long as no one figured out what they fought over, it was probably okay to let off a little steam with him.

The only other way to let off steam was kissing, but that just caused heat of another kind, making it hard to remember that everything was fake. She had to separate reality from fiction and not get sucked into believing things could be different.

They were not different.

She should have asked for twenty grand, not ten. He hadn't batted an eyelash at her demand.

Adam came toward her leading two horses. The brown one with the white mark on its forehead was Jupiter. The other one was lighter in color and taller.

Riley gulped. "That's Ladybug? I was envisioning something... dainty."

"She's gentle." Adam dropped both sets of reins and cupped his hands at Ladybug's stirrup. "Come on. I'll give you a boost."

She was going to need it. Or a stepladder. She patted the horse's nose. "Hi, Ladybug."

"You're stalling."

Yeah, she was. She planted her boot in Adam's hands and vaulted into the saddle with his help.

He adjusted the stirrups — he'd guessed closely — and handed her the reins. "How's that?"

There was only one correct answer. "Good."

Adam grinned at her, and it was as though the stern words had never been spoken. "Atta girl." Then he mounted Jupiter in one fluid motion and pointed up the dirt road past the cabins. "Let's go."

The sun touched the hills, casting shadows against the golden light. At least they wouldn't be long.

ADAM TURNED in his saddle to see Ladybug plodding behind Jupiter, Riley perched on top. He probably should have given her a different horse, but she was doing pretty well, considering her nervousness. What, exactly, did she mean by *not a lot* and *not recently*?

The trail widened out, so he edged Jupiter to one side and waited for Riley to come up beside him. "How are you doing?"

"Fine."

Her smile looked completely brittle in the waning light. She was not fine.

His fault. He'd pushed her. But what choice was there? She'd told Declan she could ride, so she'd have to make good on it.

Hmm. He'd told everyone he was marrying her... so he needed to make good on it? Was that any different? A man's word was his bond. Declan had drilled that into his head, building upon what Dad had taught him in his younger years.

He didn't want to think about the time after Dad's cancer diagnosis. All the hospital stays, the chemo, the way Dad became frailer and frailer. The way Dad's brother, Jason, had hovered around the ranch, trying to help out.

Mom had pushed her brother-in-law away, time and again.

Adam had always wondered why. With Uncle Jason's

help, Mom wouldn't have needed to marry Declan Cavanagh. Adam and his brothers could have grown up at Running Creek, and he'd never have had to fight Travis for everything he had. Noah and Nathaniel'd had the same problem with Blake, but to a lesser degree, maybe because there'd been two of them and only one of Blake.

Ryder, Declan's youngest, had been just a little kid back then. Only six years old, no threat to anyone. Everyone doted on him, Cavanaghs and Andersons alike.

It was hard to remember he'd been Adam Anderson. He should have fought harder to keep Dad's last name, but Mom insisted the adoption was for the best. Then he should have legally changed it back when he left home, but he hadn't wanted to hurt his mother. Now it seemed too late, and who cared that much? It was just a name. He could prove not all Cavanaghs were bullies.

"It's pretty up here," Riley said softly.

Adam glanced over. "Yeah, it is." So was she, not that she wanted to hear it. To her, everything was about the ten grand and the pretense that would earn it for her. She was quite convincing, especially with the kissing. At times he forgot it was all a sham.

And then her back went up like it had by the stable, and he was fully reminded once more.

Every woman he'd ever known kept a part of herself aloof from their relationships. Chantelle sure had. Turned out he'd only been her eye candy, and she'd thought that would be enough for him. It had been flattering at first. She'd sought him out after he'd won the trophy in Vegas, fully appreciative of all his masculine charm, just as he was awed by her feminine wiles and her amazing voice. She was famous! And she wanted him, Adam Cavanagh. For a while, until he opted not to jump when she snapped her fingers, and that had been the end of that.

Part of him knew Riley was not like Chantelle, but neither was Mom. The situation was quite different. Declan had done the pursuing, as far as Adam remembered, but once Mom got the security she wanted, she'd shut her husband out. Never mind that she shouldn't have married him to begin with. She'd said her vows. Adam had been there. He'd heard every word, along with five other scrub-faced boys sitting in a row wearing brand new boots and jeans and matching light blue snap-front shirts.

Women were always after something. Riley was after ten grand. He'd do well to remember that was all she wanted and not be taken in by those kisses he put on for the family. And, maybe, because he liked them.

Possibly he should do that less often. Keep it to the public moments like Riley'd asked. Because the lines in the sand were clearly marked. He and Riley had a business agreement and nothing more.

He'd only known her for two days. He barely knew anything about her other than she'd been running from something and needed cash.

She was not the kind of woman he'd marry someday before he was forty. He and Riley argued too much, but the kissing nearly made up for it.

Riley's sharp intake of breath yanked him back to the present.

He swung to see what had traumatized her, but her eyes were soft and wide as she stared ahead. "Look," she whispered.

A whitetail buck with a six-point rack watched from across the clearing. Jupiter tossed his head, and the deer took off, leaping over a fallen log and disappearing into the thicker bushes along the creek.

Reflexively, he reached for his rifle, but of course he didn't have it with him. Didn't have a hunting permit, either. Too many years away from Montana. Too out of sync with the seasons.

His mouth watered for venison chops doused with a thick layer of sautéed onions and mushrooms. Good eating.

"Are you a hunter?" Riley's eyebrows tipped upward.

"Uh... yeah?" He studied her face but couldn't figure her angle. "Don't tell me you watched Bambi too many times when you were a kid and bought into the Hollywood agenda."

"Montana born and bred. My gram used to make a mean venison stew. From deer she shot herself."

Whew. "You had me there for a minute. Do you hunt?"

"Haven't yet, but I'd be game to try. A big boy like that one, though... seems like he should run free."

"I know what you mean. You have to respect the land and not take more than you need. Obviously, we have plenty of beef, and sometimes we raise a few hogs or meat birds, but wild meat is a major bonus. Blake is an exceptional hunter, but a crew the size of the Cavanagh clan has a big appetite."

Riley chuckled. "I've noticed." Her face was cast in shadow, and the last vestiges of sunbeams slipped off her reddish-blond curls. She sure was pretty.

Adam stopped himself from sidling closer and

stretching to kiss her. He'd have no excuse out here. He kind of wished he didn't need one, but yeah. He didn't have the best track record with women, and women didn't have the best track record with him, either. Best to try to get out of this with both of them as unscathed as possible.

"Time to head back." His voice was gruffer than intended. He turned Jupiter and nudged him into a trot. Ladybug's hoofbeats were right behind him.

CHAPTER EIGHT

W ho're you?"

Riley whirled at the sound of a female voice out in the stable. A woman about her own age stood just outside the stall she'd been cleaning, studying her with eyebrows raised.

"My name's Riley—"

"So... you're the girl my brother told me about."

Her brother? Riley's brain scrambled then cleared. This was Scotty's sister. The mother of Travis's child.

"The one who enchanted Adam." The woman advanced a couple of steps, flicking long dark hair over her shoulder.

"Enchanted?" The incredulous word burst out along with a laugh. Oh, no. Better the woman thought that was entirely true. "I mean, we're madly in love, of course..." Wow, that didn't sound convincing at all.

"Can I see the ring Adam gave you?"

Riley held up her leather work gloves. "It's in my cabin. It's so big, it doesn't fit inside these. I wouldn't want to catch it on anything." Mostly because it would be worthless as a pawn item if the ring were missing its diamond or had bent prongs.

The woman crossed her arms. "I bet you don't even have one. Scotty said he thinks you never even met each other before Monday night."

"You really think I'd go around kissing men I don't even know?" Totally guilty. "By the way, I don't believe we've met. Or, at least, I missed your name."

"Dakota Erickson. Just don't let your eyes wander, Riley. Travis is mine."

If Riley bit her tongue any harder, the tip would fall off. "Oh, congratulations! I guess we'll soon be sisters, then. When's the big day? Can I see *your* ring?"

"I'm not marrying him anytime soon, but that doesn't give you the right to get between us. Travis and I have a son together."

"Adam told me about his nephew. Toby, isn't it? I just cleaned his pony's stall."

Dakota laughed. "Adam the Great's fiancée mucking out behind my kid's pony? I like it. You'll never catch me with horse manure on my boots."

"Mama? Where's Daddy?" A little boy collided with Dakota's leg and grabbed on as he looked up.

"I'm not sure." Dakota tousled the little guy's hair then looked at Riley. "Maybe this woman knows."

"Sorry to disappoint. The guys are riding fence somewhere today, but I can't tell you which guys — besides Adam — or exactly where. But I'm sure Travis won't want to miss any time with his son, so I bet he'll be around soon."

Toby leaned against his mom's leg and looked over at her. "Who're you?"

Riley squatted and tugged off her work gloves. "I'm Riley, and you must be Toby. Your uncle Adam told me about you."

"Adam is not Toby's uncle. He's just Travis's stepbrother."

Go ahead. Split hairs. Riley smiled at the boy. "He said you were a pretty cool kid."

"Look, if you don't know where Travis is, I need to find him. I have to get back to Jewel Lake. I've got a busy weekend planned."

Riley bet she did.

"Come on, Toby." Dakota took the boy's hand then turned back. "I'd just leave him with you, but that would send the wrong message."

"I've got work to do, anyway. I'll see you around, Toby."

The little boy looked up at his mom. "I play with Emma?"

"We'll see."

Riley peeked out of the stall to watch them make their way out of the stable. Dakota was something else. There'd been no need to be rude, though Adam had warned Riley there was no brotherly love between him and Travis. Still, watching Dakota swing her son's hand and laugh at something he said revealed a softer side.

What would it be like to have a child to pass back and forth every week with a man she'd once loved? Dakota was so defensive about Travis. She couldn't possibly be over him, no matter how much she blustered.

Riley pushed the wheelbarrow toward the stack of

straw bales she'd been told to use for bedding. Only one more stall on today's agenda, and that was Jupiter's. She'd take extra care on that one.

"YOU NEED TO GET OVER HER." Blake elbowed Nathaniel as the two led their horses into the corral.

Adam glanced over, his hands on Jupiter's reins. He'd been gone too long if he didn't even know his kid brother had loved and lost.

"Easy for you to say," mumbled Nathaniel. "You're not the one left high and dry."

"You don't know everything. Sometimes it's best to face the music and move on."

"Leave me alone."

"Dude, it's been months, and you haven't gone out once that I know of. No girl stays away that long if she's coming back."

Frowning, Adam followed the pair into the stable. Travis and Ryder had come in earlier, and Noah was at one of the ranches near Saddle Springs for a few days, shoeing horses. Adam didn't mind riding the south flank by himself. Gave him more time to think about what he'd gotten into with Riley. But, it seemed, he was out of touch with his brothers. Did Noah have a girlfriend, too, and Adam just didn't know?

Good thing he was back where he could keep an eye on things.

Nathaniel led Kingpin into his stall while Blake took Zorro into the one two gates down.

Adam paused and watched Nathaniel slip Kingpin's bridle off. The horse tossed his head, then accepted a slice of apple before allowing Nathaniel to secure the halter.

"Anything you want to talk about?" Adam asked.

Nathaniel glanced over. "What do you mean?"

"I couldn't help overhearing what Blake said."

"None of your beeswax. None of his, either."

"I'm back for good now, Nat. We're brothers. We're a team."

Nathaniel shoved his cowboy hat higher on his fore-head and studied Adam. "There's no teams, man. We're all Cavanaghs around here."

His voice was so bland Adam wasn't sure if he meant the words at face value or not. "Well, if you want to talk, you know where to find me."

"Lip-locked."

Adam grinned. "Not all the time. Take right now, for instance. I'm here, talking to my brother. No smooching in sight."

"Look. You got nothing to brag on, okay? You come back here like twice a year, and suddenly you show up with a fiancée that none of us ever heard of. You want a broth-erly chat by the campfire, maybe you should start by being a bit more upfront. I've been right here, working my butt off on the ranch, while you've been off amassing more belt buckles than any cowpoke can rightly wear in a lifetime. You can't just walk in and be the big brother. It's different now."

"Different how? We're still brothers."

"Didn't you hear a word I said? Blake's my brother, too.

And Ryder." Adam noted he didn't mention Travis. "Like Blake said, it's been a long time."

"She just up and ditched you?"

Nathaniel rolled his eyes. "You old hound dog, you. Just won't let up when you've caught a scent, huh?"

Adam shrugged. "I should've been here, sticking up for you."

"Dude, can we get something straight? I'm twenty-six, not a kid who needs his big bro to beat up a playground bully. I thought me and Ainsley had a good thing going. I'd bought a ring to give her for her birthday. There was nothing to tell me she was gonna ghost right out of my life, okay? Not a single clue. Trust me, I've gone back over everything a thousand times."

Adam leaned on the swinging gate and lowered his voice. "Were you sleeping with her?"

"None of your beeswax, bro."

"So, yes."

"Shut it." Nathaniel swung the saddle off Kingpin and across the rack. He grabbed a brush then began currying his horse.

This was probably not the time to remind Nathaniel how they were raised. It's not like Adam could brag about his purity, either, but after Chantelle, he'd cleaned up his act. Then Ace's accident had offered strong reminders of possible negative consequences. "They say it's guys who just want the conquest and then aren't interested anymore. They're wrong. It's gender-neutral. Women can be just as bad." Chantelle was a prime example there. At least, with Riley, Adam knew that's all there was. They were open about using each other, and no one would be hurt when they went their separate ways.

"I don't want to hear this."

"I'm sure you don't." Adam hesitated. He wanted to tell Nathaniel that God had a plan and all that. Bad timing.

"Well, take care with Riley, then. Because something tells me she's just after you for what she can get, same as your last girlfriend. She gets it, and she's gone."

Nathaniel couldn't guess how close to home he'd struck, but Adam had an image to uphold. "Naw, not Riley. She loves me." The lie sat bitterly on his tongue.

"Beware, is all I can say. I thought the same of Ainsley, and I was wrong. First chance, and she was gone without a trace." Nathaniel laughed, a bitter sound. "The Cavanagh curse. Just look at Travis."

Dakota's car had disappeared in a cloud of dust as Adam rode into the ranch yard. At least she wasn't around to overhear, and Travis was likely off with his son somewhere.

"We're Andersons."

"Tell yourself that, bro. That's not what our legal paperwork says."

Adam shrugged, and Jupiter bumped his shoulder. He should really get the gelding untacked, brushed, and fed so he could go find Riley. It was too bad they'd met under the circumstances they had. They could have hit it off and had a real thing going, but no. He was after Running Creek, and she was after money. At least it was up front.

RILEY SHOULDN'T HAVE BEEN EAVESDROPPING on the brothers' conversation. She'd known it before she sidled closer. Then she found out for sure.

Women could be just as bad, huh? Taking a guy, using him, and then discarding him? Maybe sometimes. But not the way men used women. Even this farce of an engagement fit the pattern. Yes, Nathaniel was right — though how he'd guessed, she had no idea — in that she'd gain from this relationship. But it had been Adam's idea, and he'd benefit much more if it worked. He'd gain an entire ranch, not a measly ten grand.

She should have asked for more.

But, no, she wasn't really the kind of woman the brothers had talked about. Her request had been fair in the light of giving up several months to help him, though she'd signed the papers that enrolled her as an employee of Rockstead Ranch, so she'd also be drawing a paycheck. The salary was payment for mucking out stalls. The ten grand was payment for her acting abilities, which she needed to brush up on if Nathaniel was already suspicious.

"Eavesdropping?" Blake's arms rested on the top of the gate to Zorro's stall.

Heat suffused Riley's face. "I was going to leave the stable until I realized it was a bad time to walk past them."

Blake raised his eyebrows and adjusted his cowboy hat. "Oh, yeah?"

She was terrible at lying, and now her whole life was a lie. This was ridiculous. But Blake was the last person she'd confide in. Second last. Travis would take top spot. And then Dakota. Never mind the order.

Riley smiled at Blake. Maybe it would look natural.

"Every relationship has its ups and downs, right?" How old was Blake? Had to be at least mid-twenties. "I'm sure you've experienced a few of those yourself."

He grinned and winked. "In the words of my bro, none of your beeswax."

"Um, probably right." She glanced down the alleyway to see Adam leading Jupiter toward her.

"Hi, honey." He bent and kissed her. "Hi, Blake."

All a show. Always. She'd do well to remember she was only acting a part. "Hi, babe. How was your ride?" Babe? Seriously? Where had that come from? Drama 101, apparently.

He tugged her close to his side as he led Jupiter the rest of the way to the stall she'd just finished cleaning. "Good. Missed you all day, though." He nuzzled her temple.

Heat flushed her face and tingled through her body. *Not real. Remember it's not real.* But Blake might still be watching. "Missed you, too." She ran her fingers over his scruffy jaw.

Adam's eyes darkened as he looked into her own. "Not as much as I missed you." He cupped her chin in his free hand and kissed her again, much more thoroughly.

Her knees wobbled and she grabbed at his arm to keep upright.

"Get a room," yelled Blake.

Maybe the acting was a little too convincing. Ugh. Where was the balance?

This gig was going to spoil her for another man.

CHAPTER NINE

"Y our dad goes to church?"

The sound of disbelief in Riley's voice pulled a chuckle out of Adam as he edged his truck into the lineup leaving Rockstead on Sunday morning. "Not so much."

"But..." Riley's brow furrowed as she glanced over her shoulder at Declan's truck behind them.

"I know, but it's not what it looks like. He'll drop Mom and the twins off at the church then go for coffee at the Golden Grill with his buddies. They'll discuss world politics, the price of cattle and hay, the weather, and the crutch religion offers to those who can't think for themselves. Those who are weak, you know."

"I don't understand. At breakfast, it sounded totally assumed that everyone would attend."

"That's how it's always been." Adam followed Travis's truck, leaving a gap so dust didn't billow into the cab. "I remember Declan dropping off his boys at church back when we were all little kids. His wife had left him, and I guess he needed a break from three rowdy boys, so he let the Sunday school teachers handle them for an hour or two while he went for coffee."

Riley tilted her head as she studied him. "I didn't realize you'd known their family before — well, I guess that's dumb. Of course, your mom knew Declan, and you kids knew each other. That would have been before online dating."

"Oh, I'm sure that was already a thing but, no, they met at church. She thought all he needed was a godly wife, since he obviously prioritized church attendance. For the boys, not for himself."

"It's hard to imagine them in love." Riley's eyes widened as she covered her mouth with her hand.

The sparkle of his diamond on her finger caught his attention. She didn't wear it all the time, citing how she didn't want to snag the gem on anything and lose it. Sue him if he didn't get a thrill from seeing it, though. But a ring didn't mean anything. Mom wore Declan's rings, too. "I'm not sure they were ever in love."

"Then why? I mean, I get that Declan needed help with his sons, but why your mom?"

"She was a teacher. She'd gone back to Creekside Academy when Noah and Nat turned six, but she quit when she married Declan. Then she homeschooled all six of us. We're just too far back in the hills to commute into town every day for school."

"That explains Declan, but it doesn't explain your mom."

Adam cast his mind into the past. "She's never given me a solid answer, honestly. She used to tell me she'd done it for the best, but I don't think she could say that with a straight face anymore."

"Running a ranch by herself and teaching full-time must have been a lot, though. Especially when she was mourning."

Adam scowled. "I was twelve when Dad died. The twins were nine. Between the three of us, we were the equivalent of one adult man."

Riley's mouth lifted in a grin.

"What, you don't think so? Ranch kids take responsibility young. I'd been riding beside my dad for years, ever since I'd stopped sitting in the saddle in front of him. I'd have quit school to do a man's work any time if Mom would have allowed it. She insisted on me finishing high school."

"Smart woman."

"Yeah, maybe. Except for the part where she married Declan." Adam glanced in his rearview mirror. His stepfather's truck rumbled along right behind his as though urging Adam to greater speed. Thing was, if he did go faster, he'd never hear the end of it. All applicable sins would be laid at his door, from breaking the speed limit to stirring up dust to creating potholes in the road.

"When I get married, it will be for love." Riley settled back into her seat and crossed her arms.

Adam flashed her a glance but couldn't resist the dig. "Being engaged doesn't count?"

"Fake, fake, fake." She rolled her eyes but didn't look his way. "When it's the real thing, yes, it will be for love."

She'd worn jeans and a flowered top that peeked from her down parka today. But she'd created a bun from her long curly hair, exposing her neck. She hadn't worn makeup around the ranch — at least, not that he'd noticed — but she'd applied some with care this morning.

She was pretty. Too bad they hadn't met under different circumstances, because she was a girl he could see the new Adam dating. Maybe even falling for.

What if it had been Travis in the Golden Grill last Monday evening? What if Riley'd demanded a kiss from him? Travis would have brought her home, too, mostly to make Dakota jealous.

Was Adam any better? He was also using Riley, but at least she knew it.

"What're you thinking?" Riley's brows had drawn together as she watched him.

"Thinking I'm glad it was me standing in the restaurant lobby on Monday night."

Her face flushed. "I can't believe I did that to you. I'm not usually nearly that forward."

"It was cute."

"Just what every girl wants to hear. You threw yourself at me, and it was cute."

Adam laughed. "Truth, though. And seeing Scotty come in after you sealed the deal. He's a dirt bag."

"Agreed. Is Dakota any nicer?"

The truck bounced over a cattleguard before Adam glanced over again. "You've met her, haven't you?"

"Yeah, she told me to keep my claws out of Travis, because he belongs to her."

A snort erupted before Adam could stop it. "They might deserve each other."

"But they're not together, right?"

"On and off, from what Nathaniel tells me. Mostly off."

"Poor Toby."

"Yeah, it's a rough way to grow up, but he loves it at the ranch. And Trav seems to like having his kid around. Who knew?"

"Dakota seems to be a good mom, too. She was a little snarky to me — she'd gotten the scoop from Scotty, so she was biased — but she's great with Toby."

"Good to know. I'd hate to hear his life was miserable when he wasn't at Rockstead."

"Any of your other brothers dating anyone right now?"

He flashed her a grin. "You looking?"

"As if." Riley rolled her eyes. "Just trying to figure out the things I should know about your family."

Adam thought back to the conversation he'd overheard between Nathaniel and Blake. "I think Nat's coming off a relationship. His girlfriend ghosted him. He thought they were serious — he'd even bought a ring — and then she vanished before he could propose."

Riley fidgeted and looked out the window.

He scowled. What on earth? "Ry, honey..."

"There's no need to *honey* me when no one's around, Adam." Her chin came up. "Maybe she'd learned something about Nathaniel that made her doubt him. Or maybe she'd already doubted him and learned something that solidified it. Lots of reasons could apply."

"What happened to discussing things like mature adults?"

"Some things can't be talked out."

Curiouser and curiouser. "Been there, huh?"

Something flickered across her face as she turned to

look out the truck window. "Wow, I didn't realize Jewel Lake was this big."

They'd just rounded the final curve and descended past the town's welcome sign. From this vantage point, intersecting streets formed a grid that ended at the beach along the lake, which gleamed in the late October sunshine.

"The lake or the town?"

"Either. What's the population?"

"You're changing the subject." Adam pressed the brake as the traffic light in front of him turned yellow.

"What part of town is your church?"

Yeah. She definitely didn't want to talk about ghosted relationships. Interesting.

RILEY COULD APPRECIATE GENTLEMANLY GESTURES EVEN if they were all for show. Adam opened the truck door and caught her as she slid out of the cab. His hands lingered on her waist as he brushed her lips with his own. "Ready?"

Ready for the next act in their drama. She nodded and smiled up at him as he laced their fingers together then turned to face the building across the parking lot. "It's big."

"Creekside Fellowship hosts a private Christian school. Creekside Academy is in the two-story wing."

"Crazy that Jewel Lake is big enough to support a private school."

Adam shrugged. "Some Missoula families drive their kids out here, too. It's only twenty minutes on the interstate."

Trees towered behind the edifice and framed a parklike

area to the left. It must be lush and green in summer with its large grassy area, ponds, and hedges.

She'd be long gone by then, but Jewel Lake might not be a bad place to settle after she and Adam split up. Close enough to see her sister, but far enough away that she wouldn't be in the way of Jodie and Mick's ill-fated relationship.

Riley needed to take advantage of cell phone coverage to get in touch with her parents. She hadn't said much in the quick email she'd sent a few days ago beyond the stereotypical, 'I'm fine, but don't try to find me.'

She hadn't sent Raul any messages at all. He didn't deserve one. If that made her as evil as Nathaniel's girlfriend, so be it. Raul was an opportunistic jerk. Quite possibly worse.

"Good morning, Mrs. McDiarmid. I'd like you to meet my fiancée, Riley Dunning."

Riley yanked her attention to the middle-aged woman shaking Adam's hand.

"Why, hello, honey. I'm the church secretary here at Creekside, and I'm so pleased to meet you." Mrs. McDiarmid reached for Riley's hand. "Sneaky Adam kept you all to himself, did he? Word's out now! When's the big day?"

"We haven't confirmed a date." Adam touched the small of Riley's back. "Sometime in June, maybe."

"Oh, it needs to before mid-month. We're booked every Saturday from mid-June until the end of July for the outreach, so you can't pick then. Come by the office and I'll help you choose something earlier."

"We'll be sure to check in with you before we set a firm date." Adam nudged Riley ahead of him.

"Wow," she whispered. "Is she for real?"

"We can stall her until January. Don't worry."

There were going to be a lot of disappointed people when she and Adam broke up. One of them might be Riley Dunning.

Adam escorted her into a row near the front. Too late, Riley realized that put her next to Kathryn, with the twins just beyond. Nathaniel and another man sat at the far end of the row, with Blake, Ryder, Travis, and Toby in front of them.

Seriously? Families still sat together in church like this even when all the kids were adults? She and Jodie had rebelled by the time they were Alexia and Emma's age, sitting with their giggling friends in the balcony overlooking the main sanctuary. Pastor Thompson had aimed more than one barbed sermon at the youth.

"Noah!" Adam stage-whispered down the row. "Good to see you!"

The guy at the end must be Nathaniel's twin, the only brother Riley had yet to meet. Noah grinned and saluted before Kathryn sent a pointed look to each of her sons.

Riley pulled back a smile. She could just envision Kathryn marshaling six boys by herself and doing a great job of it, even with the addition of infant twin daughters. Something had happened to snuff out her confidence and verve.

According to Adam, his stepfather had happened, like the pounding of the surf eventually eroded rocks along the seacoast. But there had to be more.

A band took the platform, and the leader invited the

congregation to worship. Adam took Riley's hand in his as they stood.

She hadn't known this guy for a full week yet, but already his warm, firm grasp felt comforting and solid. She'd kissed Adam more in one week than she'd kissed Raul in an entire year. Why hadn't she realized sooner that something major was missing?

What she had with Adam wasn't the real thing, either, even though it felt like it compared to Raul. She was some mixed up when what she knew was fake looked better than what she'd thought was real. For one thing, Adam belted out the songs, even though he wasn't always quite on key. Raul had a decent voice but mumbled the words.

Why couldn't she have met Adam like a normal person instead of launching herself at him and demanding a kiss? Even now her cheeks flushed at the memory of how forward she'd been. Yes, panic-struck with Scotty's determination she stay with him, but did that excuse her behavior?

Her mother would be mortified. Her father would be disappointed. And Raul? He'd wonder why she'd never felt that sort of passion for him, her betrothed.

She knew the answer now, but she hadn't known it then.

By the time she got to her third engagement — if she ever did — she'd be a wiser Riley.

When Pastor Marshall took the podium, Riley was ready to hear the Word.

CHAPTER TEN

L ife settled into a rhythm over the next couple of weeks. Adam's brothers had moved most of the cattle from the high meadows before he returned home. They'd shipped a couple of truckloads of calves, but Declan kept most of them back to bring to slaughter weight at Rockstead. That meant more chores over the winter, but Running Creek's vast haylands supplied the feed, and there were enough hands to do the work, even with Noah gone several days a week, hauling his black-smithing trailer around the area to shoe horses.

Adam had to hand it to his stepfather. The man was business savvy. He paid his sons fairly, offered room and board, trucks and horses, and kept Rockstead operating firmly in the black. And Declan definitely worked just as hard as he expected them to. He led by example.

Which meant he was always around. Always watching... which suited Adam just fine. His stepdad had caught him kissing Riley more than once. Adam made sure most of that was on his own time, though. He didn't want to be seen shirking his duties in the meanwhile.

It was a tough line to walk, because the more time he spent with Riley, the more time he wanted to spend with her. She was fun. She was interesting. And she was kissable.

Adam reined his thoughts in as he and Jupiter crested a rolling hill. Rockstead land flowed eastward from here, but he made out the glint of water and circle of trees that lay just across the fence line on Running Creek. The ranch once owned and operated by Joe and Kathryn Anderson.

Adam's destiny, along with his brothers. There was land enough for the three of them.

A saddle creaked, and a horse whiffled. "Wool gathering?" asked Declan's sharp voice.

Adam glanced at his stepfather seated atop his black gelding, Diesel. The man raised his eyebrows at Adam, waiting. Was this the chance Adam had been waiting for?

He nudged his chin toward the distant view. "I've been thinking about Running Creek. I'd like to make a home over there with Riley once we're married." He took a deep breath. "I think it's time my dad's land came back to his sons, don't you think?"

Silence stretched long before Adam dared look at Declan again. The man's gaze seemed to pierce his soul and bare Adam's motives and morals. "We're one family now."

"No disrespect meant, sir, but I was twelve when my father died, not a baby. I remember him well. I remember life before cancer, when my parents loved and laughed." Adam pinned a stare on Declan. Could anyone say the same of Mom and Declan, remembering a time when they operated as a loving unit? He doubted it. Even he and Riley had more going for them.

"Your father was a good man."

Adam blinked.

"Much finer than his brother."

"Uncle Jason?" They'd mostly lost touch with Jason's family after the move to Rockstead.

Declan rolled his eyes.

Of course, Jason. Dad had no other siblings, but two brothers could scarcely have been more different. Jason was a whiny man whose brassy wife had kicked him out, keeping their two daughters from him. Adam and his brothers had been much too cool to play with younger town-girl cousins. They hadn't seen much of the girls after the divorce, anyway, but Jason had come around more often.

Adam pulled his thoughts back to the topic at hand, far too important to lose focus. It was the whole reason he'd taken Riley's plea that night and upped it with one of his own. "The cabins at Rockstead aren't big enough for a family. Riley and I want a houseful of kids..."

His voice trailed off. Did she? He had no idea. But, all of a sudden, he could see a passel of them. Little girls with their mama's wild hair and smiling mouth, little boys strutting about, begging to ride like he and the twins had done. Making babies with Riley — no, he couldn't let his mind go there. Definitely not right now.

"Travis manages."

"He's only got Toby part-time, though. What if he married Dakota, and she moved to the ranch? Where would they live?"

Declan grunted.

Surely the man had considered the question. All six boys were in their twenties, Ryder just barely. Nathaniel had been set to propose. Noah claimed he was too busy to court a girlfriend, and Adam wasn't close enough to Blake to ask. It wasn't any of his business. What *was* his business was acquiring Running Creek Ranch for himself and his blood brothers.

"I know you've got the home-place rented out, but there's enough time to give them notice. We'd want to start running calves there in spring and fix up the house some. Plus, I'd like to see all the records for Running Creek since you married my mother."

Declan tugged on his black felt hat. His narrowed eyes burned holes in Adam's skull as Diesel fidgeted between his knees.

Adam lifted his chin ever so slightly and stared back. He was twenty-eight. Fully a man, and the son of his father. Declan had no right to keep his heritage from him.

"You really going to marry that girl?"

"Of course, I am." Adam spoke quickly, not allowing too much thought. "She's amazing, and we're madly in love."

"She's State Senator Dunning's daughter, isn't she? New Mexico?"

Was her dad really a politician? She hadn't talked much about her family. Very, very little, now that he thought on it. Best not to reply too directly. "She was born and raised in Montana. Her sister lives in Missoula."

His stepdad grunted again. "Spring wedding, you say? I'll consider." The man pivoted his black gelding and cantered away.

The air seeped out of Adam's lungs as he sagged in his saddle. Had that gone well? He couldn't really tell, but at least it wasn't a flat-out no. He couldn't talk to his mother about it, and had no idea if he had a legal leg to stand on if he consulted a lawyer.

Better by far if he could make a deal with Declan without involving anyone else.

Now that the picture had come in his mind, he couldn't push it out. Maybe he didn't want to. His parents had been happy at Running Creek. Why couldn't he and Riley? They may have started on an awkward foot, but was there any reason they couldn't admit they were really falling for each other?

Because Adam was pretty sure he was. The vision of Riley in the modest house at Running Creek, mothering his children, dug in and grew some roots.

He liked the look of it.

A lot.

"TELL us again how you and Adam met."

Riley leaned on her pitchfork and looked over to see the twins hanging on the gate to the stall she was cleaning. Three weeks in, and she was still on stall duty. Looked like she'd be doing that until the day she left. Yay.

But it beat recounting stories to Alexia and Emma. She and Adam hadn't crafted a super-detailed story. Enough to get by in general terms, not enough to satisfy the curiosity of two starry-eyed thirteen-year-olds.

Alexia's brown eyes shone, while Emma held back, no less interested.

"There's no time for tales. I need to get all these stalls mucked out before your father gets back."

"We'll help," volunteered Emma.

"We're bored," moaned Alexia. "Why can't we ever go to town when it's not Sunday? We don't even have hardly any friends besides each other."

The twins' life must be lonely. Riley could see that. At least they had each other. Think if there were only one of them. A solo girl in this remote, testosterone-driven place would be in far worse shape.

"Dad even fired the cowboys that weren't our brothers. And they were so cute."

"How did you know it was the real thing?" Emma begged. "Were you ever in love before Adam?"

Neither were questions Riley wanted to answer. The first, she couldn't, and the second, she wouldn't. She forced a laugh. "Honestly, girls, I have work to do."

Alexia batted her eyelashes. "What does falling in love feel like? Does it make your heart skip a beat for real, or is that just in books?"

"Having butterflies in my stomach sounds like I'd need to puke. Kind of disgusting," the other twin added.

Riley forked soiled bedding into the wheelbarrow. Maybe the girls could entertain themselves with questions for an hour or two. Maybe she wouldn't even need to reply.

Alexia tapped Riley's shoulder as she went by. "Do you stick your tongues in each other's mouths? Is it fun? Because it sounds gross."

Emma reddened and shuddered.

"Why are you asking me all this stuff? Go ask one of your brothers." Seriously. Anyone but Riley.

Alexia crossed her arms, scowling. "Travis smacked the back of my head so hard I saw stars."

"That was because you asked him if he liked sex."

"Well, I wanted to know! No one tells us anything if we don't pester them. And I know he's done it because he has a kid." Alexia eyed Riley. "Are you pregnant? Is that why you're marrying Adam?"

Riley choked on her own saliva. "No."

"Do you do sex with him?" Alexia continued. "Maybe you're pregnant and don't know it yet. How soon do you know? Like, right away?"

How had this conversation — if such it could be called — gotten so far out of hand in two minutes flat? She might not condone Travis's violent reaction, but she could understand it.

Alexia tapped on the top of the gate. "We don't know all the details, but we've figured out some things. Like—"

"Stop!" Riley held up her free hand. "That is completely enough."

"I told you," muttered Emma.

"Aw, Riley, *please*..." Alexia batted her eyelashes.

"No. You know what? Mothers are for answering questions like yours."

Emma sighed. "Ours won't talk about *anything*."

"But she's done it at least three times." Alexia leaned closer, fixing her gaze on Riley. "Twice with her first husband, and at least once with our dad."

Riley choked back an undignified giggle. Letting it out

would only encourage the incorrigible twosome. What would they say if they knew most married couples had sex considerably oftener than when they wanted to conceive? Maybe looking at their parents' strained relationship had fostered their misperception. Understandable, but Riley wasn't going to be the one to set them straight on that or dozens of other related subjects.

"There you are, girls." Kathryn made her way toward them, dressed in jeans and riding boots.

Riley had never been so glad to see someone in her life... with the possible exception of Adam that night at the Golden Grill. "Hi, Kathryn."

A warm smile crossed Kathryn's face but didn't erase the lines around her eyes. "Riley, would you like to go riding with the twins and me?"

Emma clasped her hands together and fluttered her eyelashes. "Please say yes."

She'd been riding with Adam several times now, so she wouldn't look too green. But she'd been assigned a row of stalls to clean this afternoon, and no doubt Declan's orders superseded Kathryn's. "Sorry, I can't." Riley gave Adam's mom a regretful smile. "I've got work to do."

"Dad wouldn't mind," suggested Emma hopefully.

Daddy's little princess could probably do no wrong, but that wasn't Riley's title. "In the daytime, I'm just another Rockstead employee with a to-do list."

"And in the evenings, you and Adam smooch," mumbled the other twin.

"Alexia."

"It's true, Mom! You should see them."

"You shouldn't snoop."

Excellent point taken, though. Perhaps Adam was right when he said there were eyes everywhere. He might not have meant his twin sisters... but maybe he had.

Kathryn turned to the stall across the alley. "Saddle up, girls. We'll invite Riley to ride with us another time, after clearing it with your father. It looks like we'll have rain for a few days after this, so we should get going while the weather holds."

The twins jumped off the gate and raced each other to the tack room.

"I'm sorry if they were bothering you."

Their mother had no idea... unless she'd been listening for a few minutes, and Riley didn't want to think about that possibility. "It's all right. They're just curious teens who don't get out much."

Oops. Hopefully that hadn't sounded like censure.

Kathryn grimaced. "This ranch is so far from Jewel Lake. It's not like we can just drop into town anytime."

"Less than an hour." Not by much, though.

"Each way. And then they want all day to hang out with their friends. It's too far to come home in between."

Surely Kathryn had friends of her own to visit? But maybe not. Maybe not friends who'd stuck with her through her fifteen-year marriage and isolation.

But Kathryn didn't seem a prisoner. She could get away if she wanted to. Maybe she really loved Declan.

Asking personal questions of Adam's mom sounded too much like the twins poking at things Riley wanted to keep private. She'd never make Kathryn that uncomfortable.

"Mom!" yelled Alexia.

"Excuse me." Kathryn strode away, her boots clicking on the alley's hard surface.

Riley watched her go, leaning on the fork as her brain rattled through the barrage of questions.

What does falling in love feel like?

She'd thought she was in love with Raul, but then it shouldn't have been so easy to walk away from him when his true colors became apparent. She hadn't mourned anything but her own stupidity for believing his lies.

Adam, though? She didn't dare fall in love with him. Their relationship was clear. They'd play their parts. He got a ranch. She got ten grand. Then they'd part ways. Falling in love wasn't an option.

But she couldn't help wishing.

CHAPTER ELEVEN

Adam stared at his email inbox with its list of unread messages. He really should check it more often. The one from Sawyer Delgado was an auto-open. His buddy still hadn't convinced his pregnant ex-girlfriend to marry him. Next on the list was one from Mrs. Desjardins. Adam was in no hurry to open that message... but maybe Ace was improving? Maybe he'd woken from his coma after five weeks and was sitting up, laughing and eating.

A man could hope.

Adam tapped to open it and scanned the message, his heart sinking. Ace was *not* improving. He hadn't so much as twitched his big toe in all this time.

The memory of all the wires and tubes and monitors attached to his buddy's body assaulted Adam. Accidents like Ace's were rare in rodeo. By the time cowboys reached the pro circuit, they'd learned to tune out everything else for that eight-second ride. They didn't always make the time. Adam'd had a few broken bones and more concussions than he could rightly remember, but nothing life-threatening.

There was no way to prove that Vanessa's announcement about her pregnancy and her attempt to extort money from Ace before he rode had affected his focus, but it had to have. Ace was a pro, easily best in class.

The last lines of the email caught Adam's attention, and he reread them.

Vanessa has been such a comfort. I can only pray Ace awakens soon and marries her, providing a home for his baby. I know that's all he'd want since he rededicated his life to the Lord.

Was it Adam's duty to burst Mrs. Desjardins' bubble and tell her Vanessa was a conniving cheat who was actually responsible for Ace's condition? He remembered Ace's mom kneeling at his hospital bedside, holding her son's hand, pleading with God to save his life. Ace was her only child, all she had left after her husband's death. She'd been ecstatic when Ace came back to his childhood faith earlier in the fall. She envisioned great things for him.

Would he live to do those things?

Adam shook his head. The dimness of his vision might have as much to do with tears trying to multiply as with reliving those memories.

He wouldn't be the one to tell Mrs. Desjardins. If Ace revived, he could do it. If he didn't — Adam didn't even want to think about that — then maybe the knowledge wouldn't matter anyway.

"Adam? Are you okay?"

He turned toward the doorway to the rest of the house to see Riley standing there, her head tipped to one side as she studied him.

"Not really." He took a deep breath. "My buddy Ace — still no change. How long do they keep someone on life support if there's no improvement?"

"I'm so sorry." Riley came toward him, holding out her hands.

Adam caught them and tugged her to his knee. He wrapped his arms around her and buried his damp face in her neck. "Why would God let something like this happen, just when Ace had rededicated his life to Him?"

"I don't know." Her fingers massaged the tense muscles of his shoulders. "Sometimes life just doesn't make any sense at all."

The sadness in her voice caught at his heart. He didn't know much more about her past after several weeks than he had the first night. What he did know was her sweetness and her tender heart. Not for the first time, he wished they'd met a different way, that he hadn't jumped the gun with a fake proposal. He'd likely ruined any chance of something solid happening between them.

But she was just here for the money, and because she'd needed a safe place to land for a while. Why? He still didn't know. He'd never found a good way to ask, and it probably wasn't any of his business, anyway.

It wasn't like they were really a couple... though it would be very easy to forget that right now with Riley perched on his knee, pressed against his chest, with her arms around his neck. This went beyond putting on a show in case someone came past the open office door. She really felt like she belonged in his arms.

Maybe... maybe she did. Maybe he could redeem their spontaneous meeting and his outrageous request. Maybe she was coming to see something more in him, just like he was seeing it in her.

Adam lifted his face from the damp spot on her shirt collar and studied her. Her gorgeous blue eyes, her unruly hair pulled back into a messy ponytail. He traced the tiny freckles dotting her cheek with one tentative forefinger.

Their gazes locked. Held. Then her lips curved upward, just enough to give him courage.

He pulled her closer — how was that even possible? — and caught her lips with his. "You're amazing," he whispered.

Riley's eyes darkened as her arms tightened around his shoulders. And then she kissed him back.

It wasn't their first kiss, not by a long shot. It also wasn't the first one to stir Adam's heart and soul. But something new had passed between them. An understanding of more than a mutually beneficial pact.

There might be hope here, hope for something real and true. He wouldn't rush it with words, though. Not until he was sure it belonged to both of them.

He trailed kisses over her tiny freckles and back to her mouth.

"Are they doing the thing with their tongues?"

"I can't tell for sure."

Riley jerked out of his arms and shot to her feet, her eyes wild as she took in his sisters, who stood much too close. How had they snuck up on him and Riley? And what on earth were they doing, discussing kissing techniques? They were thirteen!

He pointed at the door to the kitchen. "Get out."

Alexia crossed her arms and raised her chin. "You can't make us. This is our office, too."

"Yeah." Emma peered from behind her twin. "We wanted to check our email."

"But you're blocking the computer and sitting in the best chair. I think it's you who should get out." Alexia looked between him and Riley.

Adam spun the chair and logged out of his email before surging to his feet and grabbing Riley's hand. "Maybe we will."

Riley was flushed from the kissing. He probably was, too, but all he wanted was to hold her close and do it some more. Somewhere without an audience of impressionable girls barely in their teens.

"What's it like?" Alexia's voice was full of curiosity. "It looks kind of gross, so what's the big deal?"

A snort-laugh erupted from Riley, and she dragged him out of the office and through the kitchen and dining room to the foyer.

A cold wind cut through Adam as they stepped out onto the covered porch.

Riley shivered. "Brr."

"I'll warm you up."

She shrugged away. "Back to your best behavior, cowboy."

"Promise." The moment might be broken, but he could still tuck her close to his side as they walked back to the cabins. But going inside together might not be the best idea. Not tonight, when his emotions were barely under control.

Those twins!

Riley gathered her wits around her along with her down jacket as she stood on the steps to her own cabin, the cold wind whipping at her.

What had just happened in there?

She'd known since that first night that Adam was a good kisser. He'd obviously done a lot of it. The celebrity singer was not likely his first girlfriend. But there'd been something about this kiss in the office that came from a deeper place.

Now he stood two steps below her, waiting for her to go inside. He sometimes came in, just as she sometimes entered his place several doors down. It didn't look like tonight was going to be one of those evenings. She wanted him to, desperately, which made it a bad idea.

Probably her desperation had showed in the way she kissed him, and now he was taking a step back. To him, it was all a show. She kept forgetting that, especially when he looked at her with such tenderness. The cowboy should be in some Hollywood movie with that level of fakery. He'd be the swoony heartthrob of every girl in America.

"You okay?" Adam still stood on the walkway, hands shoved deep in his jeans pockets.

Riley managed a chuckle, hearing her words to him from a few minutes ago echo back at her. "Peachy."

His eyebrows rose, barely visible in the glow of the amber lightbulb beside her door. "I was wondering..." His words hung in the air for a long second.

It's a game, Riley. She lifted her chin. "Don't overtax your brain, cowboy. You might need those half dozen braincells someday."

Adam's mouth quirked into a lopsided grin. "Half dozen? You're being generous after all my concussions."

Whew, she'd dissipated the mood. Maybe now she could breathe. "Concussions, huh? That would explain a lot."

He looked away then back at her, his jaw ticking. "I should go. We've got a long day tomorrow. There might even be snow in the high country. Rain at best."

"Guess I'm on stall duty again."

"Want to ride out with me? I can ask Declan."

"Then who'll shovel manure?"

"Ryder. Or maybe it's time the girls learned. They obviously need something to occupy their minds besides wondering how kissing works."

Good thing it was dark out and she stood with her back to the light, because her cheeks heated again at the memory. "They've asked me stuff like that several times before."

Adam tipped his hat back. "They have?"

"Yeah, sometimes they hang around and watch me work and pester me with questions." Riley hesitated. "They seem a bit obsessed with kissing."

"Think I should talk to my mom about it?"

"They don't really listen to her."

"They don't listen to Declan, either." Adam shook his head. "I could try telling them it's not appropriate."

Riley scoffed. "That will go over well. They'll just take their questions to the internet. They may have already."

She could just envision the search terms: *what does it feel like to kiss?* Or, *what do tongues do when you're kissing?*

Yeah. There was no way she was interfering, one way or another.

"I like kissing you, Riley," he said softly.

"Easier to convince your family, then." Except she shouldn't say things like that out loud, outside, even though no one seemed to be around.

"There's more to it."

She needed out of here. "You keep telling yourself that. I need my beauty sleep so I can look my best for the shovel and wheelbarrow in the morning." She faked a yawn. "Good night, cowboy."

"Good night, honey."

Riley closed the door against his quiet endearment then leaned her head back against the wood panels. What had happened to the loud, confident cowboy she had no trouble resisting? Okay, that was a lie. He was irresistible in any guise, but this tender side had nearly undone her tonight. She'd have gone anywhere with him in those brief moments in the office before his little sisters had so effectively doused them both with figurative ice water. Riley, at least. It seemed like Adam was still under the spell.

That's all it was. He'd read something in that email that had made him sad and vulnerable. She'd come along and held him. Comforted him. Sometimes human contact from someone who loved — er, cared about — a person made all the difference. Riley wasn't going to read anything into it. She was too smart to be taken in.

Raul had faked some good vulnerability a few weeks ago, too, pretending she hadn't caught him kissing Maggie

Sanderson. It wasn't like Riley thought, he'd insisted. Maggie had flung herself at him and kissed him, and he'd been taken aback. Didn't know how to get out of it quickly enough.

Raul lied. Riley had watched for over a minute before shoving his shoulder and breaking them up. He'd definitely been giving as well as he'd received. She hadn't even needed to see the flash of guilt in his eyes or notice that Maggie had slipped away leaving him to face the music on his own.

Guilty.

Plain and simple.

What did Riley and Maggie have in common? Fathers who had a lot of political influence. Raul was covering all his bases. Literally.

Adam was a whole lot sweeter than Raul from everything she'd experienced with both of them. But, even though her heart seemed to be falling for the suave cowboy, her head grabbed the knowledge that they'd made an agreement.

He was only playing a part. Convincingly, yes, but still acting.

She, on the other hand, was starting to tumble into the fantasy. She could envision a future where they actually loved each other, had kids together, rode out on Running Creek — their own ranch — together.

Fool, Riley. He's got a lot to lose if anyone suspects the truth. You're just a pawn. Don't forget it.

She tugged off her down parka and hung it on its hook before prying her cowboy boots off her feet. She added a couple of split logs to her little wood stove, trying not to think how Adam brought in a few armloads for her every day.

Tonight would be a great night to surf the web, but it was not to be. No way was she going back to the main house. Instead, she'd pull up a book on her ereader and get lost in a story.

It might be best if she read something besides romance. Something with no kissing.

CHAPTER TWELVE

T hanks for taking time for me, son."

Adam kneed Jupiter up beside his mother's horse now that the trail had widened some. "My pleasure. I don't feel like we get a lot of time together." At least not where he felt comfortable speaking his heart. Who knew if Declan had bugged Mom's suite? Probably not. That would require him to consider there might be something not-quite-perfect going on in his kingdom. Although a guy would think having one's wife live on a different level of the house than he did would be a pretty big clue. That had happened after Adam left Rockstead, but his brothers had let him know. They'd helped with the construction.

"It's a beautiful day after all that cold rain."

"It is." Had they gone for a ride just to discuss the weather?

"Your fiancée is a lovely girl. I'm so happy for you both."

Adam shifted in his saddle. Man, he hated lying to his mother. But maybe it wouldn't end up a lie? Because he was starting to feel something new for Riley. Something akin to hope. Something he dreamed might be reciprocated. "She's great," he said at last.

"Have you talked to your stepfather about Running Creek?"

"I have. He was noncommittal, of course."

Mom nodded, her lips tight as she stared straight ahead.

"Why did you sign everything over to him when you married him?" The question burst out, but better this one than the one about why she'd married him at all. Mom and Declan hadn't ever even tried to convince anyone of their deep love. Not like he and Riley were doing... and apparently succeeding at.

"It was for the best."

Adam clenched his jaw and shook his head. "Could you dispense with the brick wall and help me understand what happened back then? Because *for the best* doesn't cut it. I'm twenty-eight, Mom. I deserve real answers."

If he hadn't been watching, he wouldn't even have noticed the quick, tight shake of her head.

"You can't say it's none of my business. You signed away my inheritance."

"Declan will do what's right."

"You have a lot more faith in him than I do. He completely brushed me off with that old 'I'll think about it' line. Like he hasn't had fifteen years to figure out his plan. Or like it's all up to him and not up to you as well. It was *your* ranch. Yours and Dad's, and you just gave it away."

"Ours and the bank's," Mom corrected, still not looking at Adam.

"Lots of people have mortgages." Wait. Did this mean

Declan would expect Adam and his brothers to pay him for what he'd invested in Running Creek? Adam grimaced. That would probably be fair. Not that Declan needed the cash. Well, Adam had money in the bank, even after he paid Riley off. Noah was making a steady income as a circuit farrier. Nathaniel might have been saving, too, if he'd planned to get married. Maybe the three of them could pull it off, regardless of the strings Declan attached.

"This is true, but it did affect my decisions. Your father's life insurance didn't cover everything, not with all his medical bills."

"Surely you had options besides Declan."

"I did, but his was the best offer by far."

"So, you married him and signed Running Creek over to him, even though you didn't love him." Not that this was a huge shock. Adam had never seen any evidence of love between them. Just a marriage of convenience which turned out not to be all that convenient. Maybe things had been better in the early days. After all, Alexia and Emma hadn't come from thin air.

"Your father was my one great love, Adam. I loved him like you love Riley. We..."

Her voice may have gone on. In fact, it probably did, but she'd lost him when she'd mentioned Riley and one great love in the same context. What did she see when she watched them together? Because he and Ry had visited her a couple of times a week, so she'd had chances to observe.

"What do you see in us?" he blurted out. Oops, he'd interrupted her with no idea where her words had gone after that bombshell.

Mom pivoted in her saddle and stared at him from

beneath furrowed brows. "You and Riley? What do you mean?"

"Do we look happy?" He didn't want to put doubts in her mind, not this early, and especially not if she and Declan ever talked things over. They must, occasionally, right?

"Do you look *happy*?" she repeated, her voice incredulous. "Adam, honey, I've never seen you so settled. So content."

"I feel that way," he admitted. "But remember I've also rededicated my life to Jesus in the past few months. Pretty sure that has a lot to do with it." In fact, he knew it did, because *that* was real while the thing with Riley was not.

"I'm not discounting that, son. But I also see the way you two look at each other, as though your beloved has hung the moon. It does my heart good to see the stars in your eyes when you look at Riley. When I see the way you naturally protect her with an arm around her shoulders or just by taking her hand."

It's all a sham, Mom. All fake.

It had been. But was it still?

Mom chuckled. "I'll admit I had doubts at first. Last I heard, you were coming off a relationship with that singer. The next thing I knew, you were bringing home a girl we'd never heard a thing about, telling us all you two were engaged. You've always been impulsive, but this was a whole new level."

Yeah. About that.

"But since then I've watched the two of you together, and it's done my mama heart good to remember young love. You've resurfaced good memories of the early days with your dad. Before you boys were born. Before cancer swung its wrecking ball through what seemed to be a perfect life."

Adam opened his mouth, couldn't think of a thing to say, and shut it again. Either he and Riley were both much better actors than he'd thought, or there was really something there between them. It almost seemed too much to hope for after the rough beginning.

Finally he swallowed hard. "I'm glad you like her. I can see what you mean about it seeming to be sudden but, as soon as we met, I knew there was just something about her. Didn't take me long to decide I needed to pursue her in a big way." Like five minutes, tops.

Mom smiled, but it didn't quite reach her eyes. "I'm truly happy for you, Adam. She's wonderful, and she's good for you."

Their split-up would crush his mother. His rash proposal back in October had been just that. But maybe there was hope. Mom corroborated what Adam had been seeing and feeling on his own.

There was definite potential for something long-term with Riley.

"THEY'VE STILL GOT you mucking out stalls?" Dakota sounded more curious than contemptuous.

Riley straightened and glanced over to the woman leaning against a squared timber post. "Sure do!" She didn't mind. Not much, anyway, since it kept her out of Declan's line-of-sight for most of the day. She was pretty sure if he spent too long staring at her, every one of her secrets would be laid bare for all the world to see.

"Mr. Cavanagh can be a hard taskmaster."

"Yes, but he's fair." Riley'd seen that for herself, time and again. She worked hard, but she'd received two paychecks now, and both were in the bank. He assigned the men fairly, too, playing no favorites.

"I bet you can't wait until Adam takes you away from here, though. Or is he going to work for his stepfather forever?" Dakota's eyebrows arched.

Like there was any way Riley was going to confide in Travis's ex. "We're examining our options. We're in no hurry."

Dakota forced a laugh. "I thought you weren't sleeping together."

"We're not." Not that it was any of Dakota's business.

"Then seems like there might be some pressure. You haven't even set a firm wedding date!"

"Maybe early June. We'd talked about later, but Mrs. McDiarmid says the church is booked every Saturday from mid-June through July. They've got some big outreach rally going on next summer."

"Oh, I heard about that. An eight-week geocaching hunt. They're calling it Pot of Gold." Dakota shook her head. "They think locals will participate and even tourists will flock in. Bummer it interferes with your wedding plans, though."

"Kathryn suggested if the wedding were small enough, we could have it in her garden instead of the church."

"That would barely hold the Cavanaghs, let alone your

side of the family. I mean, it's nice, the few glimpses I've seen of it through the gate. Kathryn's never invited me in."

Shouldn't surprise Riley. Travis showed his contempt of the Anderson side of the family as much as Adam felt it for his stepbrothers and stepfather. And Dakota was even further removed since she and Travis weren't actually dating at the moment.

Riley pushed her cowboy hat back a little. "Where's Toby?"

"Emma met us at the car when I drove in and offered to watch him until Travis came in from the range. What are the guys doing today?"

"Fencing on the northern perimeter, I think." She'd learned to note their duties on Fridays, since Dakota never failed to ask.

"Are you going home for Thanksgiving? I asked Travis if I could keep Toby that weekend for my family's sake, but of course he refused." Dakota made a face.

"No, I'm staying here." Truth be told, Riley hadn't even thought about the upcoming holiday. She talked to her mom for a few minutes most Sundays between church and lunch at the Golden Grill. Creekside Park by the church had decent cell coverage except for being a little spotty where the creek tumbled through a small canyon. Riley had learned to wander that direction so cell service would be disrupted, and she could beg off from the call.

She hadn't even told her parents about Adam or her engagement, fake or otherwise. Dad would immediately talk to Raul, who'd try again to contact her. Best leave him completely in the past.

"Aw, your parents will be disappointed, I'm sure. Where do they live again?"

Riley eyed Dakota. There was no *again* about it. She'd never told the other woman anything personal. "Too far for a casual visit, sadly." Or not so sadly.

"Somewhere south of Wyoming, I'm guessing." Dakota chuckled.

Right, she was Scotty's sister. Scotty knew that much.

Riley checked her watch. "Wow, I'd better get going here. The guys will soon be back, and I've still got one more stall to clean."

"You work too hard."

"It's what they pay me the big bucks for." Riley laughed. Okay, the big bucks were for acting, but at least the pay for cleaning stalls was steady and sufficient. Maybe after she and Adam broke up, she could find work on another ranch. There was a guest ranch not too far away. Sweet River might be hiring come spring. She'd done more riding lately, and she'd begun feeling more confident in her abilities.

"Sometime when you come into Jewel Lake, we should hang out. Go for a movie or something."

Define 'or something.'

Riley shook her head. "I don't have my own wheels, so I don't really go anywhere without Adam."

"I could pick you up when I drop off Toby some Friday afternoon."

An actual overture of friendship? Or was there more to Dakota's offer? Maybe she figured if Riley had too much to drink she'd start spilling her secrets. Nope. Not happening. "Thanks for the thought, but I don't think that will work.

You'd have to give me a ride both ways, or Adam would need to come get me. That's a lot to ask of anyone."

"Maybe sometime."

"Maybe." She didn't want to alienate Dakota, but a heart-to-heart? Nope. She wasn't seeing it.

"Anyway, I'd like us to be friends, since we're both tied in with the Cavanagh family."

How could Riley reject that out of hand? She couldn't, so she offered a smile. "Sounds good. I can always use another friend."

What she really needed was a friend who wouldn't stab her in the back, and she wasn't completely convinced Dakota Erickson was capable of that.

Time would tell.

CHAPTER THIRTEEN

A dam, would you ask the blessing?"

Adam's gaze snapped to his stepfather's. Eyebrows raised, Declan stood at the head of the table with the golden turkey in front of him, ready to be carved. The whole family, dressed up in their Sunday-go-to-meeting clothes, sat in their usual seats around the resplendent table. Staring at him. Even Mom was here today.

"Sure." He cleared his throat and closed his eyes. "Dear heavenly Father, thank You for the many blessings You've given to each and every one of us. Thank You for sending Your Son to die for us and offer salvation. Thank You for supplying everything we need, for keeping us healthy..." His mind shot to Ace for a few seconds before he pulled it back. "We ask Your blessing on this meal and our time together. In Jesus' name, amen."

Riley squeezed his knee under the table.

Declan narrowed his gaze at him, but more thoughtfully than antagonistically. Then he picked up the carving set and began to slice into the bird.

Mom looked around the table. "While your father carves the turkey, why don't we take turns letting everyone know what we are thankful for this year? Alexia, go ahead."

Alexia rolled her eyes. "This year is just like every other year. We never get to go anywhere or see anyone. There's nothing to be thankful for."

Emma jabbed her twin's side with her elbow. "*I'm* thankful for Desiree. Thanks, Dad. She's a great horse."

"Oh. Yeah. Same with Domino. Thanks, Dad. I like her."

Declan grunted something that might have been acknowledgment as he laid another slice of white meat on the platter. The aroma of the roasted turkey mingled with the other dishes on the table, causing Adam's gut to grumble.

Riley's fingers laced with Adam's. "I'm thankful to have met Adam this year. And thankful for all of you, for welcoming me to Rockstead."

Adam knew his cue when he heard it. He leaned over to press a kiss to her temple, just long enough for one of the twins to giggle. "I'm thankful for Riley. She makes my life complete." Not quite as complete as getting his hands on Running Creek, but far more than he'd expected a month ago when they'd met in the Golden Grill.

Declan paused carving for a few seconds. "I'm thankful for good calf prices this year and healthy stock."

Travis was thankful for Toby, Toby was thankful for Toy Story, and the other brothers' replies were rather vague. Nathaniel's jaw was set as he mumbled something about good fall weather. Seriously?

When it came back to Mom at the foot of the table, she smiled at Adam. "I'm thankful to have my eldest back in the fold, for his regained faith, and for his lovely bride-to-be."

He hate-hate-hated to deceive his mother, especially with the realization of how much she'd suffered from depression the past few years. Having Riley here had given her something bright to focus on, and Adam was going to yank that away from her as soon as he and Declan had settled things with Running Creek.

He was such a heel and a liar to boot. How could he claim to have revived his relationship with Jesus when he lived a lie every single day?

Blake plopped a huge mound of mashed potatoes on his plate and passed the serving dish to Ryder. Emma and Alexia squabbled over the bowl of dressing.

Riley pressed her shoulder against his arm. "You okay?" she whispered as the hubbub picked up around the table.

This woman. Her sensitivity to his moods knew no bounds. Her blue eyes studied him.

"Better now," he whispered back.

Her mouth lifted in a little grin, and he fought the urge to kiss her right at the dinner table. It wouldn't have been for show, either. It would have been because he really appreciated her. Maybe even liked her a lot.

Too early for love, though, right? But it didn't feel like it. He'd dated plenty of buckle bunnies in his day, women who hung around pro rodeo to snag attention from macho cowboys and be seen with them. The more trophies and buckles he won, the more attention he received. He'd simply accepted it as his due. A mark of success.

And Chantelle Devereaux had been the most insidious

of them all. She'd been his arm candy there for a few weeks, just as he'd been hers. What an idiot he'd been.

When would he be done using women for his own advancement? He was doing it again with Riley, but she wasn't like the others. She didn't deserve what he'd thrust upon her. Sure, she'd come willingly... he still didn't know what that was all about, but he was one hundred percent certain he hadn't forced her.

The family dug into their turkey dinner, quieter than usual. Maybe it was because they normally discussed the day's work, and today they'd done the minimum of feeding the livestock. All the family members had cleaned their own horses' stalls this afternoon, giving Riley the day off as well.

It would have been a party in the stables if Nathaniel hadn't been so glum. He'd barely said even a word to his twin, even though Noah usually brought him out. Maybe they'd done all their talking in the cabin after Noah arrived late last night from his weekly farrier rounds.

Not for the first time, a tinge of jealousy curled through Adam at the thought of what his twin brothers shared. Maybe if he'd stayed at Rockstead instead of chasing rodeo dreams, they'd have been a tighter threesome, but he doubted it. Noah and Nathaniel had been a unit from birth. He'd always been the outsider.

As he listened to Alexia and Emma whisper on the other side of Riley, he was thankful anew that his sisters had each other. Imagine a solo girl with all these big brothers. It was bad enough with the two of them.

"I'm so glad you could stay for Thanksgiving." Mom

leaned toward Riley. She smiled, but the lines on her face and the shadows beneath her eyes belied any true joy.

Adam could only be thankful his mother had made the effort for this family meal. He could count the times she'd been present in the month he'd been home.

Riley sent a fleeting smile. "Thanks. Me, too." Then she took a big bite of salad.

It'd never mattered too much what Riley was running from. He couldn't imagine anything too insidious, but maybe he did need to find out. He couldn't make the leap from fake to real without knowing more about her.

"Your family's loss is our gain." Mom glanced at Declan then back at Riley.

Adam dared a peek at his stepfather. Declan didn't look up, but his fork paused for a brief instant in midair. What was that all about?

And then there was Riley, not responding.

He took another bite of roasted Brussels sprouts. Was the tension in the air real? He'd never had that good of an imagination. If he felt it, it existed.

Huh. Did that go to his developing feelings for Riley, too? Were they real, or were they simply a natural outcome of so much acting?

"DRAW FOUR." Riley slapped the Uno card on the table and eyed Adam around the corner on her left. What colors had he played lately? "Let's make that blue."

His eyes glittered. "Don't start with me, woman."

"Too late," she said sweetly.

Noah guffawed. "She gets you every time, bro."

Adam glanced at his brother as he picked up the extra cards. "You want to reverse play so I can get her back?"

"Nah, I'd rather get Nat with a Skip. Don't worry, Nat. If I had a Draw Four, you'd be getting it. Your turn again, Riley."

"Thanks a bunch." Nathaniel glared at Noah.

"Oh, look. I have a Skip, too. Back to you, Noah." She batted her eyelashes at Adam. "Sorry, cowboy."

"Lying doesn't become you, woman."

Except it kind of did. Wasn't this whole thing a farce? Sure, hanging out with Adam and his brothers didn't mean anything on its own, but it was one more little thing grafting her into this family before she pulled up the tiny roots.

She didn't want to walk away. Not that she wanted to keep shoveling out stalls for the rest of her life.

"Have you taken Riley down to Running Creek yet?" Noah asked when play had settled into a less vindictive routine.

Adam shook his head. "I don't want to freak out the renters poking around like I own the place."

Nathaniel grunted.

Noah wasn't around much, but he seemed friendlier than his twin. He shook his head and slapped down a card. "Declan hasn't given you the go-ahead yet, Adam? I was sure he'd give in right away when he found out about you and Riley."

Adam sighed. "Me, too. Also, Draw Two."

Riley held her breath.

Noah picked up the extra cards and glanced at his

brother. "At first, I'll admit I thought you were playing a tough game with our stepdad. You know, faking him out."

"At first?" Adam's voice was steady.

"Well, you've got to admit this whole thing with you two seemed to come out of nowhere. You might have known each other a while, but nobody told the fam."

Should she say something? Anything? No, better leave it to Adam. These were his brothers.

Adam's hand found her knee under the table, and Riley dared to breathe. "After the Chantelle disaster, I wanted to be really sure before I went public with Riley."

"Makes sense. Chantelle was a fiasco for sure."

Riley really needed to dig into his relationship with the famous singer. Would he tell her if she asked? Did she actually want to know? Probably it didn't matter, anyway. This was all temporary.

"Uno." Nathaniel slapped a card on the table and raised his eyebrows at Riley. "And Draw Four."

"Hey, no fair!"

Adam busted a laugh and reached across the table to knock fists with his brother. "Good job. Way to get her."

"You're supposed to be on my side, not consorting with the enemy!"

He shook his head. "Says the girl who's given me every nasty card she could find. And don't pretend otherwise when you reversed play my direction and *then* doled out the Draw Fours."

She turned to Nathaniel. "Which is kind of true, so why are you picking on me?"

"We brothers stick together." Nathaniel's gaze was sharp, no teasing evident.

Riley suppressed a shiver. She would definitely not still be Nathaniel's friend when this was all over. Good to know.

Noah gathered the cards at the end of the round and shuffled them. He glanced at his twin. "Thought I saw Ainsley in Saddle Springs last week."

Nathaniel's head swung to face his brother, and his eyes narrowed. "And...?"

"Sure looked like her. I called her name, but she didn't turn around, so I crossed the street to catch her."

Riley noticed Adam was just as riveted as Nathaniel. So was she.

Noah dealt piles of seven cards. "Is she a twin? Because there's no way Ainsley could have faked not recognizing me. No spark, no nothing."

"She's not a twin." Nathaniel bit the words off.

"Then she's got a doppelgänger. Well, with shorter hair. And, um, pregnant."

Nathaniel choked, his eyes wide. "Pregnant?"

"Not Ainsley, dude. This girl who kind of looked like her. I'm sure you wouldn't have given her a second look, or at least not a third one. You'd have known right away it wasn't her. I didn't know her nearly as well."

"She ghosted me because she's *pregnant*?"

Noah laid his hands flat on the table and gave Nathaniel his full attention. "Didn't you hear a word I said? It wasn't your ex. I said, 'Hi, Ainsley,' and she looked at me oddly and said, 'You must have me mixed up with someone else.' And I realized she was right. Uncanny likeness, though."

Nathaniel jammed his hands through his hair, and his

cowboy hat tumbled to the floor behind him. "She's *pregnant?*"

Adam exchanged a worried look with Noah. "Bro, listen to the whole story."

"You don't understand. She doesn't have a look-alike."

"My sister and I share a strong resemblance," Riley offered.

Nathaniel zeroed in on her. "Enough someone would think she was you?"

"For a few seconds, maybe." Not likely, though.

"Yeah, and I only talked to this girl for like a minute," said Noah. "I shouldn't have said anything about it to you."

Nathaniel pushed back his chair and towered over them, fists on his hips. "What's she doing in Saddle Springs?"

Wow, he was fixated. He'd totally missed the point of Noah's story.

"How far along?"

Noah held up both hands. "How would I know? Not *huge,* huge, but big enough I'm pretty sure she wasn't just overweight. But listen to me, Nathaniel. It doesn't matter, because it *wasn't Ainsley.*"

"Is it my baby? Or did she run away because she'd been two-timing me?"

Noah smacked the table and shook his head. "I give up."

"Nobody's that good an actor," said Adam. "There's always a tell if someone is lying."

"Yeah, that's why I wasn't sure about you and Riley. It seemed fake at first." Noah surged to his feet, frustration lining his face. "Look, all I'm doing tonight is putting my foot in it. I'm out of here. Good game, guys, Riley." He tipped his hat to her as he turned to the door.

"I'm going, too." Nathaniel grabbed his hat off the floor and followed his twin out the door.

Riley let out her breath in the sudden silence. "Well. That was interesting."

"Yeah. I wonder if it was true?"

"What do you mean? You think Noah made the story up?"

Adam shook his head. "No. I'm wondering if she was really Nathaniel's ex or not. He seems so sure."

"He wasn't there," Riley pointed out.

"True. Still mighty strange."

Riley gathered the cards into a pile and slotted them back into their box. "What was all that about being able to tell if someone's faking it? It was like you were giving your brothers the chance to decide *we* were fake."

He grimaced. "I thought of that too late. But I've always been able to tell if someone's lying."

"Well, that's dandy. Your brothers are already suspicious. Your stepfather watches everything I do. Your mother is blind to everything but hope, and your sisters just want to know what kissing is like. Now you're giving them ammunition."

"I did not." Adam rose and pushed in the chairs. "It was a deflection. Nobody would say something that brazen if he had something to hide."

"*You* have something to hide. You think your brothers are denser than you?"

Adam narrowed his gaze at her across the table as he

leaned on the back of Noah's chair. "What're you saying, woman? Calling me dumb?"

"Not even, cowboy." Riley stood, grabbed her parka, and shrugged into it. "Just saying we're in way over our heads here, and it's only been a month. You need to get what you need from your stepfather before someone figures all this out." She tugged up the zipper and reached for the door. "Good night."

CHAPTER FOURTEEN

They were in the same booth at the back of the Golden Grill as they had been the night they'd made their deal. After church, they usually sat at one of the long tables in the middle with all the brothers and a few friends.

Adam didn't have any friends left around here. He'd never integrated much with Jewel Lake after moving to Rockstead. He hadn't attended the local high school, mostly coming into town for gymkhanas. At those amateur horsemanship events, he'd left other wannabe cowboys in the arena dust, no love lost either direction.

When he hit pro rodeo, Sawyer Delgado and Ace Desjardins had become the brothers of his heart, the best friends he'd ever had. He'd finally found a place to belong, a place where his skills had been celebrated, where everyone liked him. So, he'd put on a front. Didn't everyone?

Even Riley.

He studied her across the table as she polished off a

chicken-fried steak. They'd been together every day for going on two months now, and she still evaded questions about her past.

Just as he'd been evading questions from his mom and brothers. "Want to have a look at Running Creek today?"

She blinked at him, her fork with a forkful of green beans paused in midair. "I thought someone lived there?"

"Yeah. Declan has the home place rented out. You know, the house, yard, and outbuildings. Rockstead runs the ranch land."

"Won't the renters think it's weird if someone comes in the yard?"

Adam hesitated. "Heard at church they're away for a couple of weeks. Mrs. McDiarmid said Hawaii."

She put the vegetables in her mouth and chewed while staring at him thoughtfully. "Okay."

"Good. Want some cheesecake?"

Riley shook her head. "I'd kill for a gooey chocolate brownie, though. You'd think a diner like this would serve something other than cheesecake for dessert."

"It's a Golden Girls diner." Adam waved his fork to direct her attention to dozens of photos and memorabilia from the classic sitcom on display.

"Right, whatever, but—"

"Look, I've never seen but two episodes in my life, but apparently cheesecake was a serious thing on the show, and Estelle plays everything as close as she can."

Riley's eyes widened. "Golden Grill. Golden Girls."

"Uh, yeah. Anyway, you want some brownies, we can grab a box from Super One. The bakery is closed Sundays. Or I'll tell Cook you want some. She's certainly up for it, and the twins would probably love you forever. What's up with women and chocolate, anyway?"

"Hormones." She ate the last few bites of her steak while he cleared his plate of mashed potatoes and gravy.

The only hormone Adam knew much about was testosterone. Without a hefty dose of it, guys would have enough sense to avoid high-risk sports like bronc riding. He'd thought it was the greatest way to live until Ace's accident. Now, it looked anything but.

They turned into the lane at Running Creek Ranch a half hour later. The home place sat much closer to the highway than Rockstead's did, and the whole setup was less imposing. The two-story farmhouse lacked the grandeur of Rockstead's mansion but, to Adam, it looked far homier. The barn and stables were smaller, but they'd been big enough for his dad. That made them good enough for Adam.

A dog ran from the house toward them, barking his fool head off.

Adam frowned. Had the rumor been wrong? Maybe the renters weren't on vacation, after all. Either way, he and Riley wouldn't get out of the truck. There wasn't any need to trespass on the folks' privacy.

"It's nice." Riley peered out the truck windows. "Is that the same creek that goes through Rockstead?"

He shook his head. "No. Different source."

"What a pretty house. I like the wide, covered deck."

"There was a porch swing when I was a kid." Adam's voice thickened at the memory of his parents sitting out there, shelling peas, talking about their day, while he and the twins climbed that big elm to the treehouse. With the branches barren at winter's approach, the old platform was clearly visible, but the walls were gone. He'd rebuild it for his sons.

But even that thought threatened to choke his air supply. Would Riley be his sons' mother? Maybe it was time to lay out his cards and let her know he was actually falling for her. Find out if she felt the same, or if there was any hope she'd come to.

A truck growled up the drive behind them.

Oh, no. Caught sitting in someone else's yard. Adam could always pretend he'd lost his way. At least he hadn't shut off the engine or gotten out. He shifted into drive and pointed the truck back toward the driveway.

Scotty Erickson's blue pickup lurched around the curve.

Great. Just whom Adam wanted most to see. He tipped his hat and turned the wheel to maneuver past, not that the guy had left a ton of room.

But Erickson's window came rolling down as he pulled even.

Until he knew why Scotty was at Running Creek, Adam couldn't be rude enough to edge past without exchanging pleasantries, so he put his truck in park and pressed the button to lower his window. "Erickson."

"Hey, Cavanagh." Scotty peered past him and his jaw ticked. "Riley. What a surprise."

Adam leaned his elbow out the window, thankful for his shearling-lined denim jacket. The early December afternoon had a distinct bite to it. "Not sure why you're surprised. We're engaged, after all. I think you knew that."

Erickson snorted. "Didn't believe you for a minute. Still

don't, all evidence to the contrary." His gaze narrowed on Riley.

"Well, believe it."

"Riley, if you think better of hitching your wagon to Cavanagh's, you know where to find me. I'll get you away."

"Are you proposing marriage to an engaged woman, Scotty Erickson?" came Riley's light voice from beyond Adam.

Adam wasn't looking, though. He didn't dare take his eyes off the scum.

"Marriage? Isn't that a bit old-fashioned?" Erickson chuckled.

Adam's fingers clenched. Wouldn't he just love to punch the guy's lights out?

"Oh, I don't know," Riley went on. "A church wedding is every girl's dream, complete with the white dress, the flowers, and the music. The whole works."

"Yeah. Not buying that."

"Maybe that's why you haven't found a woman who'll have you, whereas I have the best one in the world right beside me."

Erickson shook his head. "What're you doing here, anyway? It might have been your old man's ranch once, but it's not anymore."

Adam tightened the reins on his temper. "It's Cavanagh land. But I could ask you the same. What brings *you* here?"

"Friends of mine rent the place. I'm looking after the dogs and horses while they're away. And I don't remember inviting you."

Didn't that just figure?

"So you might want to be on your way before I phone

the cops. I might let them know you're holding her under false pretenses while I've got them on the line."

The impulse to close the gap between the two trucks and grab Erickson by the front of his fluffy jacket was nearly too strong for Adam to resist. Instead, he offered his most threatening glare.

"Save it, Cavanagh. And get off this property."

Blood thundered in Adam's ears as his finger stabbed the button. The window rolled up, cutting off Scotty's voice. Adam muttered a few choice words under his breath as he shoved the truck into drive and hurtled around the first bend.

"It's sweet of you to get so upset, but it's okay. I promise I won't call Scotty when we break up."

"That's not what I'm frustrated about."

"Oh?" Now she sounded bewildered more than humored.

"I'm not worried about you. I just hate the thought of him in my childhood home, doing damage just to spite me. He'd do it, too."

RILEY TIGHTENED her arms around her belly as Adam took the bumpy driveway much too quickly. There was a short reprieve on the smoother highway before he turned up the much longer Rockstead drive.

His jaw remained clenched as he stared straight ahead, both hands on the wheel.

Well. She knew where she stood for sure. He wasn't concerned about Scotty's veiled threats at all. For Adam, it was all about Running Creek. She'd known that all along, but she'd begun to think she meant something more to him than a means to an end.

She'd been wrong.

Everything was a game with one single payoff at the end. Her only job was to make Declan believe they were in love so he'd deed the ranch to Adam. That's what she was getting paid for. Nothing more. Nothing less.

They jounced around the final bend to the house in record time, Adam still silent and stewing.

Riley'd had enough. "Let me off at the house."

"The house?"

"Yeah. I'm going to check my email before everyone else gets back from town."

Adam shrugged. "Sure. I'm taking Jupiter out for a good run."

In this kind of a mood on this kind of a day? "Don't break your neck."

He offered a sharp laugh. "Afraid you won't get your money if I'm dead? Explain it all to Noah. He'll pay you out."

"Like I care about that."

He hit the brakes in front of the house. "Nice try. I haven't forgotten why you're really here. See you at supper."

"Be that way." Riley unbuckled, shoved the truck door open, and slid down.

"Be *what* way?" He sounded genuinely dense.

It didn't require an answer. She slammed the truck door and hiked for the house without a backward glance.

In a few seconds, she heard the spatter of flying gravel as he revved away.

Wow. Temper, much? And all that over a rundown house and a few outbuildings? So they were his dad's. She got that. But it was still just a place. Nothing that important in the grand scheme of things.

Riley let herself into the house, threaded through the quiet kitchen, and sat down at the computer in the office beyond. She needed to keep in better touch with the outside world. Definitely needed to plan where she'd go and what she'd do when she left Rockstead in a month or two.

She navigated to her email account then scanned the list of senders, her gaze catching on Raul's name. What did he want? And, more to the point, who'd passed on her email address? He'd never needed it since they'd texted between dates back in Santa Fe.

With a trembling hand, she opened his email.

Hey, Riley!

What's this I hear about you being engaged to some cowboy not a week after throwing my ring in my face? Your parents finally heard that from your sister. Not from you. Were you two-timing me the whole time? Did you think you were too good for me? Does the cowboy know what you left behind in New Mexico?

Raul

She hadn't given Adam's name to Jodie, had she? She was pretty sure she hadn't. She'd mentioned the ranch was nearby. *Think, Riley. What else did you tell her?*

Nothing that would bring Raul to her doorstep, she was pretty sure. Unless he could geolocate her by her phone calls to her parents on Sundays after church. Did she have locations turned off? She'd make sure.

That would send Raul to the church's doorstep, not hers, but it wouldn't take long to track her from there. Mrs. McDiarmid was the biggest gossip in town. The church secretary was so tickled that Riley had captured Adam Cavanagh, there was no way she wouldn't share the information.

She snorted a bitter laugh. Adam had gone all caveman with Scotty. He could certainly send Raul back to New Mexico with one perfectly placed punch. But, what if Adam wasn't at the ranch? He spent hours every day riding the range, checking fences, keeping an eye on the weather and the cattle for the right day to shift the herds closer to the home place.

Maybe it was time to take him up on the offer to ride with him. He'd said Declan could assign Ryder to the stables. Or, everyone could clean their own if they came back in half an hour earlier. Daylight hours were scarce this close to the winter solstice, and the stable well lit. It could work.

Yes, she'd ask Adam for the chance... but could she do it without getting his suspicions up, especially after their chilly drive today? Maybe he was about to send her packing anyway. But, no. As much as he wanted Running Creek, he wouldn't let go of Riley until he had the bigger prize in his grasp.

He still needed her.

She'd ask.

CHAPTER FIFTEEN

For someone who'd begged Declan to let her ride out with the guys, Riley was sure quiet. Gone was the teasing between them. Gone was the kissing, too. Oh, she still allowed him, but her enthusiasm was down about nine notches.

Today she was riding with Travis. She hadn't batted an eyelash at Declan's assignment, but Travis had smirked at Adam. It had never occurred to him that bringing Riley out to Rockstead might result in her finding one of his brothers more attractive than him. Of course, just because they rode together today didn't mean they were smooching behind a sweeping cedar. Riley had some principles.

Yeah, like she'd thrown herself at Adam in the Golden Grill. That had been principled. Not so much.

Nathaniel edged Kingpin up beside Jupiter. "You look like the dog barfed in your breakfast."

"Funny."

"Wasn't meant to be."

Adam shrugged. "Erickson is camped out at Running Creek, looking after the place for the renters."

"He's friends with the Samsons? Interesting."

"He's an idiot. Who'd want to be his friend?"

"Who cares?" Nathaniel shook his head. "He's probably got a good quality or two somewhere."

"I care. He threatened to call the cops on me just for sitting in the truck in the driveway."

"He was trying to stick in your craw. And it worked."

"He told Riley he'd help her get away from me."

His brother's eyebrows shot up. "Now we're getting to it. Why would Riley escape, let alone need an accomplice? Trouble in paradise?"

Not compared to Nathaniel getting ghosted by his girlfriend. Riley wasn't even Adam's real fiancée. Everything was fake. "Just Erickson being stupid. His specialty."

"Then why aren't you laughing it off?"

Good question. Why wasn't he? Because... females. "Ever notice women just use men to get what they want, then they ditch them?" Too late he remembered Nathaniel's story about Ainsley.

Nathaniel's brow furrowed. "Riley broke up with you?"

"No." Not yet, anyway. And wasn't Adam supposed to be in control of the demise of their relationship? Fake relationship. He didn't have what he wanted yet, and that was Running Creek. After his parents' ranch was in his hands — his and the twins' — then Riley could do what she liked. Until then, they had a deal.

"I am so not following you."

"Forget it. Just saying she shouldn't be laughing and chatting it up with Travis. He'll rub that in later."

"Man, you are super insecure. Anyone can see Riley's totally into you. And if she's going to marry you and live here, isn't it good if she gets along with the entire family?"

He'd thought Riley was totally into him, too, but that was last week, and this was now. He'd begun to actually fall for her.

First mistake, obviously.

Nathaniel huffed. "Listen to me. You've got to stop thinking about us versus them. Declan's fair. He doesn't favor his sons over us. We all get our share of the crap jobs. We all get the same pay and benefits."

Adam turned a glare on his brother. "I don't want his favor. I want Running Creek, free and clear, for you, Noah, and me. Declan wants to show me fair? That's how. Not because Travis has cleaned the same number of stalls I have." Which wasn't true, anyway. Travis had mucked out way more stalls at Rockstead than Adam had. He'd been the steady firstborn, unlike Adam, who'd jaunted off to join the rodeo.

"Running Creek is small potatoes compared to Rockstead."

"You'd sell out your soul for a bigger ranch divided more ways? I don't get you."

"Dude. I'm not selling my soul. Do I wish we could have grown up at Running Creek as a happy family without Dad's cancer? Just been next-door neighbors to the Cavanaghs? Of course, I do. But these are the cards we've been dealt. Our dad died. Our mom married Declan. It's how it is."

"Our mom's seriously depressed, and your girlfriend ghosted you. You'll just sit back and take it?"

"Isn't that biblical?"

"I don't know where in your Bible you read that. A man sees injustice, he should meet it head on. Conquer it. Make the world a better place." Was that what he'd been doing in rodeo? Or should he have stuck it out at Rockstead and challenged his stepfather head-on all those years ago? Nah. He'd been a kid, barely green-broke himself. He'd had to grow up, become a man, before he could do that, but he was here now.

Nathaniel shook his head. "Sometimes there's just nothing a guy can do, bro. Sometimes you just have to get on your horse and do your job. You can't solve the world's problems, but you can feed the cows and keep the mountain lions away. That's pretty much what David did in the Bible. I think the Bible teaches that we have to be faithful in the little things before we can be trusted with the big ones."

"David was a king in waiting." And since when was Nat the one parroting Bible stories?

"Yeah, that's my point. But he didn't try to grab it ahead of time."

Adam shook his head. Why could Nathaniel not understand? He exhaled a long breath and watched the fog dissipate from it. For an instant it clouded the view of the December landscape. Snow covered the distant peaks in Glacier National Park, but in the lower foothills, they'd yet to have snow that stuck. There was a rugged beauty to the stark evergreens, the creek dodging around black rocks as it made its way downstream.

"There is a time for everything," Adam quoted at his

brother. "A time for life. A time for death." And that only sent his memory back to Ace Desjardins. Was it Ace's time to die?

Was it Adam's time to gain Running Creek? It seemed a petty question next to Ace's, yet Ace had encouraged Adam to go for it. Life could change in the blink of an eye.

Here today, gone tomorrow. That was in the Bible, too, wasn't it? It had to do with the flowers of the field or something. Fleeting like Ace's virility or Nathaniel's lost love.

Adam shifted in his saddle and looked at his brother. "Tell me about Ainsley?"

RILEY'S BACKSIDE was finally getting used to long days in the saddle. Adam saddled Ladybug for her every morning and untacked her every afternoon, but she rode with whichever brother Declan assigned her to.

The rancher probably figured if she and Adam were assigned together they'd spend all their time kissing instead of working. Little did Declan know that there wasn't a lot of hanky-panky going on for him to be concerned about. Now was when Riley's acting abilities were put to the test. It was embarrassing to realize how little pretense it had required to play Adam's doting fiancée for the past weeks. Now Adam's smile seemed forced and his embraces shorter and less passionate.

Good thing she'd talked herself out of believing anything further could come from it.

She'd seen Adam's face today when she'd been assigned to work with Travis. Boy howdy, that had not gone over well. What was wrong between the two of them, anyway? Were they simply vying for position? She couldn't see it, but then again, who knew with guys? Adam obviously had a lot of competitive spirit. Look how well he'd done at rodeo. Just because Travis had been the brother who stayed home didn't mean he was any less competitive.

Riley had found it easy to chat with Nathaniel, Blake, and Ryder on the days they'd worked together, but Travis only offered terse directions then pivoted Lancaster away. Because she was Adam's. But there had to be some way to get him to loosen up.

She nudged Ladybug up beside Travis where he sat overlooking the valley. By the flick of his eyes, he was counting heads. When he finally nodded, she was ready. "Are you looking forward to having Toby for the weekend?" It was Friday, after all.

Travis sent her a questioning look. "Always."

"It must be hard handing him back and forth." Now, why had she said that? She'd planned to get him to talk about his son, not about the strained situation between him and the child's mother.

He shrugged. "Yeah, but if I had him all the time, it would be hard to get any work done around here, and Dad does not like a shirker."

"I bet he doesn't." Riley offered an understanding grin. "He runs a tight ship, but he's fair." Ugh. The best she could say about the rancher was fairness? Sad.

"He is." Travis hesitated, looking like he was deciding whether to say more. "He's good with Toby, though."

Riley hadn't noticed. "That's cool." Somehow she couldn't imagine the no-nonsense man reading stories to a little kid. Grandparenthood wasn't a side of Declan Cavanagh she'd ever considered.

"Toby's pretty awesome. Dakota does a good job with him."

He didn't even sound bitter. Riley snuck a peek. He looked more pensive than grouchy. "She seems pretty nice."

Travis swung to meet Riley's gaze for a few long seconds. "Oh, yeah?"

"She seemed prickly at first, but she nearly always stops to visit for a few minutes now when she drops Toby off." Speaking of which, she'd miss seeing Dakota today. Riley'd always been on stall duty before this week.

"Yeah, she gets prickly, all right."

"How'd you guys meet?" Riley held her breath. He was going to tell her it was none of her business, and he'd be right.

"She was a barrel racer in our high school gymkhanas, not that we went to public school. Kathryn taught us. But we still drove into Jewel Lake for sporting events or church activities. Youth groups."

"Your dad took you?" Hopefully she'd kept the surprise out of her voice.

"Him or Kathryn. But then Adam got his license. And even before that, sometimes he or I would drive as far as the highway, and a friend would pick us up."

Somehow Riley wasn't too shocked to think of underage drivers on the ranch lane. She'd lived in rural Montana herself as a teen.

Travis had opened up more than she'd expected. Maybe

she shouldn't push it, but somehow she couldn't help herself. "You still care about her?"

He pierced her with a cold glare. "This is your business how?"

"Not at all," she replied glibly. "Just trying to get to know the dynamics, since I'm marrying into the family."

Travis snorted. "Or you're just nosy."

She met his gaze, trying to read him. "Maybe?"

He rolled his eyes. "Nah, Dakota can date anyone she wants. No big deal, so long as she doesn't try to separate me from Toby. Then there'd be war."

"Kids benefit if their parents are together. One family."

"What's it to you? Your parents divorced? Because mine are. We survived just fine, thanks."

"Because your dad married Kathryn?"

"Right." His disgusted grunt belied the word. "She'd have been okay, I guess, if she hadn't come with three brats of her own. But we were doing fine with Dad before she came."

"How old were you when your parents split up?"

"Eleven. Your parents together?"

"Yeah, but they fight all the time, only not in public. There they put on a happy face for the world to see." Riley'd sometimes wondered why Mom put up with Dad. Seemed she got something out of their weird relationship, too. Just another case of a couple using each other for their own gain.

"My parents, too. It was nasty at home. Even that huge house wasn't big enough to keep from hearing them yell and listening to things crash. Turns out it was mostly my mother throwing things."

Riley shuddered, imagining three little boys cowering in their closets.

"One day she up and disappeared. She left a note on the kitchen counter. I found it before Dad. Not much explanation, just that she'd had enough, and the divorce papers would be along shortly. Oh, and the postscript, telling Blake and Ryder and me that she loved us and wished us well."

"Ouch."

"Yup."

"Have you ever heard from her?"

"Via the grapevine. The papers arrived. Dad signed them. Then we never mentioned her again, but Mrs. McDiarmid down at the church let it slip that Mom remarried a few weeks later and moved to Missoula. Just like that."

"That's gotta hurt."

"And that's why I couldn't trust Dakota as far as I could throw her. It's better for Toby to go back and forth than to have to suffer like I did when one parent walks out on him. There's no way it would be me, though. I'd stick through anything to keep my family together."

Ladybug plodded along beside Lancaster, but Riley doubted Travis saw the forest around them any more than she did. "You love her."

Travis shrugged. "Doesn't much matter how I feel, does it? She's on her own path. And don't go telling her we had this talk. I'll deny every word."

"Promise." Not that Riley knew what to do with the information anyway. With any luck, she'd be away from

Rockstead in just a few weeks. Then all these cowboys would just be a blip in her memory.

All those passionate kisses from Adam? She'd pack them up and keep them in a special box in her heart. Adam Cavanagh would be someone to measure future relationships by.

And that just made her want to cry.

CHAPTER SIXTEEN

T here was a message for you on the house phone." Cook looked up as Adam passed through the kitchen. "A Mrs. Desjardins."

Good news about Ace or bad? Adam closed his eyes for a minute. "Did she give any indication...?"

"All she said was 'he's gone,' but I couldn't make out what she meant. I did leave the message for you to listen to."

He's gone. Cook's other words drifted away.

Adam felt the blow like a kick to his gut from a wayward bronc. "I'll listen to the message and call her back."

If only he could go back in time and pray that day turned out differently. But if he could do that, he'd also pray his dad's cancer away. Accepting the ways of life and death was brutally hard at times.

Riley's presence registered by the scent of her shampoo as she stepped up beside him. "You okay?" Her hand rested gently on his arm.

"No." He shrugged her away. "I have to make a phone call." He strode into the office, shut the door, and sank into the swivel chair with his head in his hands.

Why, God? Why take Ace? Why didn't You answer our prayers? It wasn't just Adam who'd prayed. Ace's mom. Sawyer Delgado. Others. Was this to punish Adam for forgetting his friend's plight for hours at a time? For finding comfort in Riley's presence and kisses? For lying about her?

God wouldn't be so cruel. He didn't take people for a friend's misdeeds. Adam hadn't caused the accident, though he'd benefitted from it. That stupid trophy languished beneath his bathroom sink behind a stack of towels. He never wanted to look at it again. He had not won that thing fair and square. It was forever marked with Ace's blood.

Now his own life was in pieces. He'd blown it with Riley somehow last weekend, something to do with Scotty Erickson. He hadn't figured out exactly what, but it didn't even matter. Riley was taking her cues from him. She'd been after some money and a place to hide out for a while. That's what he owed her. That's all she wanted. Nothing more. Nothing less.

The rest was an act, just like he'd requested. She was good at it. A career in Hollywood awaited her if she cared to turn her attention in that direction.

The phone sat on its charger staring back at him. He tapped the code to retrieve the message and listened to Mrs. Desjardins' broken message.

It was true.

Ace had gone on to his reward. His story was over.

Adam punched in her number and waited while it rang.

"Adam? You got my message."

His voice choked. "Yeah. I did. I'm so sorry."

"Me, too. I'm trusting God knows what He's doing."

"I'm trying to." How was it that Ace's mom was comforting *him*? Shouldn't it be the other way around? "Listen, if you tell me when his funeral is, I'll do my best to be there." He hadn't thought that through, but he'd still go. Declan would have to understand. So would Riley.

Mrs. Desjardins shared the details she'd already determined and said she'd be so grateful if he came. She'd love to see him again. Him and Sawyer.

Sawyer.

Adam hated making that call nearly as much. This all seemed so final, but there wasn't anything he could do about it. He punched in Sawyer's number, half hoping he could leave a voicemail, but no. His buddy picked up.

A few minutes later he and Sawyer had made plans to fly out of Missoula for Ace's funeral. Adam got online, bought the tickets, and sent the info through to Sawyer's email. His friend would reimburse him, no problem.

Ace's accident replayed in Adam's mind. He bent over the desk and cradled his head in his arms. Ace had lived as big as he could. That hadn't always been a compliment, but Adam and Sawyer had done the same. Lots of women. Lots of swagger. Lots of media attention. They'd lapped it up, but they'd been talking recently, realizing they'd made a mess of things. Vowing as brothers to change and hold each other accountable.

Then Vanessa had dropped her bomb. She was pregnant, and she was going to make Ace pay.

A few minutes later Adam had ridden a solid 82, easily one of his best scores of the season. Good enough to beat Sawyer's average. Good enough to challenge Ace's best. He'd socked Ace's shoulder. "Beat that."

With his usual good humor, Ace had laughed in his face. "Easy as stealing candy from a baby." Then he'd slid onto Cramer's back in the chute, marked out, and shot out the gate to his destiny.

He'd lasted all of three seconds before Cramer made an insane series of jumps. Ace's head cracked against the horse's rump in a hollow thud Adam would never forget. Ace slid to the dirt, and Cramer turned on him. Sharp hooves pummeled Ace's body before the pick-up cowboys could intervene and drive the bronc to the gate.

The arena was absolutely, horribly silent as the medics ran out with a stretcher and knelt beside Ace's still body. Then the sirens broke the hush.

That's when Adam had become aware of Sawyer beside him, his mouth open, his expression contorted. Adam saw himself reflected on Sawyer's face. How could this happen?

Oh, sure, they knew the dangers. They'd all taken so many tumbles they'd lost count years ago. But this, this was different.

The contestants had gathered in small groups, worried over Ace, waiting for the organizers to decide what to do. The signal had come to resume the rodeo, but no one was particularly into it. The fans' reactions were halfhearted at best. Not a single rider stuck the eight seconds to challenge Adam's early score. Sawyer had only made five.

Adam won the coveted trophy. His dream come true but, oh, so tainted.

And now Ace was gone.

Yeah, Adam would go to the funeral to pay his last respects. And if there was anything he could do for Ace's mother, he'd do it. No questions asked.

RILEY STARED at the closed door to the office. Adam had just received bad news — she'd overheard Cook's message — then pushed Riley away. Didn't he know he needed her?

She wrapped both arms around her middle and paced into the breakfast room before turning back to the open kitchen with the closed office door off to the side.

"He'll be all right, missy." Cook filled a huge pot of water at the sink in the island facing her.

Would he? She'd asked Adam a couple of times about the missing trophy. His face had completely blanked as he looked through her. "It should've been Ace's." He hadn't told her a lot about the accident, just enough for a rough picture.

The trophy hadn't appeared in its case. She'd kept an eye for it, but never mentioned it again.

Riley looked at Cook, who'd turned the faucet off and stood watching her across the island. "I don't know what to say to help him."

"Sometimes there's nothing to say. Sometimes a body just needs to get through something on their own, with only God to help."

She knew about that. Wasn't that what she'd decided in New Mexico? That she couldn't trust anyone but herself and maybe God? Yeah, she'd hitchhiked, but she hadn't let her guard down with any of the drivers who'd picked her up. Only Scotty seemed to think she owed him something further for the ride.

And then she'd prayed a desperate plea in the parking lot of the Golden Grill and taken a chance on the first man she'd seen inside the door.

Adam Cavanagh.

What on earth had come over her? Could she blame God for answering her prayer when she had literally thrown herself at the hunky cowboy? Maybe she could. The method was unconventional, but Adam was a hundred times more of a gentleman than Scotty. From the first second, she'd known she was safe with him.

Bodily, yeah. Her heart? Not so much.

Cook turned to set the pot on the stove. "Are you a person of faith, missy?"

"Yes." But didn't a person of faith actually trust God to lead her, guide her, care for her? All that seemed to be part of the package. Riley had gone from jumping on the man himself in the diner lobby to jumping at his offer to jumping to conclusions that the fiction had become reality.

She'd gone and fallen in love with the rodeo cowboy. It was easy to believe it was real when he kissed her. When they talked and joked and laughed, but it was all part of the facade.

When it really counted — when a guy would open his arms for his fiancée's comfort, he pushed her away. Right. She knew it was an act. Now she just remembered it again.

He was in it for the deed to his dad's ranch.

Period. Full stop.

She was in it for the fresh start, far from Raul and her

parents. Next chance she got, she'd start looking around Jewel Lake to see what the apartment vacancy rate and the job market were like. It was a pretty town, nicer than most she'd seen, but she'd need to be careful not to blow their cover before the public breakup.

That couldn't be too long coming, could it? Surely Declan would relent soon. After all, everyone commented on how fair he was. Hard, but fair.

The office door flew open and the knob smacked the wall. Adam exited, his face set in stone. He glanced her way without so much as a flicker of recognition or emotion. With Cook crossing the kitchen aisle, Adam routed to Riley's side of the island.

"Hey," she said softly. "Want to talk about it?" A girl had to try, especially with an onlooker.

"I'm flying to Amarillo on Monday. I'll be gone all week."

Riley realized her jaw hung slack and snapped her mouth shut. "Amarillo?"

"Ace Desjardins' funeral is Wednesday."

"Do you want me to come?" Amarillo was far enough from New Mexico there was little chance of running into Raul.

Adam gave his head a quick shake. "Sawyer's going with me. I told you about him."

"Sawyer Delgado?" He was the third in their three-some, a cowboy from over near Saddle Springs. Adam had told her very little about anything to do with his rodeo days.

"Yeah. We're meeting in Missoula."

"Okay." Riley's arms wrapped around her middle. If

Adam wouldn't hold her, she'd have to hold herself. "I'll miss you."

"Ditto." He strode across to the foyer. A moment later the outside door slammed shut.

Ditto? That's all he had to say? She'd been trying to hold things together in front of an audience, but not him. Well, it would be his loss.

She met Cook's curious gaze. "Men."

Cook shook her head then glanced around before leaning toward Riley. "I'll tell you something." Her voice was soft. "The Cavanagh boys don't know how to feel healthy emotions."

What was Riley supposed to say to that?

"He's come a long way, Adam has. You've been good for him, but he's got to process this in his own way. He'll come around. You'll see."

How much did Cook notice, anyway? Would she ever talk to Declan or Kathryn about their sons?

Riley studied the woman for the first time. She'd been a background figure, keeping food on the table, keeping the house picked up. Riley had only been thankful she hadn't had to do it. "How long have you worked at Rockstead?"

"A long time now. I've seen a lot in my day."

"How long?"

Cook took a few things out of the cupboard. "Since Monica left."

Monica. That was Declan's ex, right? His sons' mother?

Riley slipped onto a seat at the island. Adam said he'd been thirteen when his mom married Declan. He was twenty-eight now, so... fifteen years. And Cook had been here longer than that. Huh.

She watched the woman measure and mix for a few minutes. "I don't even know your name. Why does everyone call you Cook?"

"My name's Cathleen Cook, and it was just too awkward for the boys when Kathryn came on the scene. It was easiest to default to my surname, since that's how they thought of me, anyway." Cook chuckled, shrugging. "I've answered to worse."

What made a woman — Riley made a quick guess — of sixty-something live and work at a ranch with only Sundays off? Especially for a tough, no-nonsense man like Declan?

It was probably none of her business. It's not like Riley wanted anyone snooping into her own reasons for being here.

CHAPTER SEVENTEEN

Adam locked his emotions away and threw himself into his work over the weekend. He rode hard, wishing it were summer when the daylight hours were twice as long. He polished saddles and mended tack. He avoided everyone, not just Riley.

Nathaniel's mood matched Adam's, albeit for different reasons. Nat didn't ask a lot of questions, and Adam had forgotten what he wanted to know about Nat and Ainsley. Declan allowed no booze on the ranch — his father had been an alcoholic, and he had no patience for it — so Adam and Nathaniel played incessant games of cards late into the night, a small fortune passing back and forth between them.

A fictitious one, of course. Just like his relationship with Riley. If he kept on like this, their breakup would be a natural outcome of Adam's grief over Ace. For now, he just needed to hang on until he'd been to Texas and back. Then they'd figure out the next step.

Christmas was coming, right on the heels of his and

Sawyer's return flight. A guy would never know from decorations or music or dinner table talk at Rockstead. Declan wanted his sons to go to church to learn morality, but he had no use for emotional religion. The birth of a baby meant to save all humanity definitely fell into the latter category.

Adam didn't feel like Christmas, anyway. Why had God taken Ace? It was like He was allowing evil to win.

By the time Adam hugged Mrs. Desjardins in Amarillo Monday evening, he was a wreck from too little sleep and too much thinking.

"Adam." She touched his shoulder. "Ace has gone to a better place."

Adam shook his head, tears threatening to leak from his eyes. "I don't know how you can say that. He was much too young to die. Far too much to live for."

She smiled sadly. "His baby. Vanessa."

Adam exchanged glances with Sawyer. How much to say? Would she even believe them? But it was too late to overthrow the judge's decision. Vanessa had somehow proved in court that she and Ace had entered an informal marriage. She carried Ace's child — they'd run a DNA test to prove it — and the baby was Ace's heir. Vanessa would make good use of that inheritance in the meanwhile, no doubt.

Just the thought made Adam's blood boil, but was there any point in stirring things up? Maybe Mrs. Desjardins could win Vanessa over by her unrelenting faith and good nature.

He wasn't counting on it.

"Won't you boys stay with me?"

Adam shook his head. "Sawyer and I booked rooms near the arena. I'm sure you've got family coming in."

"But..."

Sawyer gave the older woman a side hug. "We don't want to get in your way."

"Don't leave without saying goodbye. When is your return flight?"

"Friday morning. We need to head to the airport fairly early, though."

"Come for dinner Thursday?"

Adam glanced at Sawyer. "We can do one better. Let us take you out for dinner that night."

"I'd like that," she said wistfully.

"We should get going. If there's anything you need help with while we're here, anything at all, you've got our numbers. We'd be happy to help."

"You're good boys. Such good friends to my son."

Emotion wrapped its bony fingers around Adam's throat and threatened to strangle him. "He was the best."

Was. Man, it was hard to think of Ace in the past tense. It seemed he should be bursting through the back door into the kitchen any second now, finger-pointing fake pistols at him and Sawyer. *Gotcha.*

But there was no reprieve, just his mama putting on a brave front while tears puddled in her eyes. "Could we pray together before you go?"

Adam managed a single word. "Sure."

Mrs. Desjardins' voice broke as she prayed God's guidance and solace for them. Wasn't it supposed to be the other way around? Weren't they here to help comfort a grieving mom?

A few minutes later Sawyer started the rental car, and they pulled away from the curb.

"Where to?" Adam didn't feel like sitting in the hotel room. He was too restless.

Sawyer raised his eyebrows at him across the car. "Jewelry store."

"Seriously? I thought Anna was still putting you off."

"She is. But maybe she just needs to see how serious I am."

"What will you do if she says no? Texas is kind of far from Montana to return a ring." Adam didn't want to think about Riley pawning his, but she would. She'd been clear from the beginning. Maybe Sawyer would just write the money off as a loss, like Adam had.

"You missed something in there, dude. I'm not giving up. Anna is carrying my baby."

Adam leaned back in the deep seat. "You can't force her."

"Who said anything about forcing her?" Sawyer navigated the few blocks to a major street and turned toward the city center.

"Do you even hear yourself?"

"How can it not be God's will for us to be a family? To raise our son together? Yeah, so we messed up big time in June. I was cocky and full of myself, but I've changed. She's changed. We're both trying to follow God's ways. So, I repeat. How could His will be any different?"

"You've got logic on your side."

"I know."

"But who knows what goes on in a woman's mind? What's holding Anna back?" For that matter, what was holding Riley back? Adam needed to do some delving of his own, but it was easier to push Sawyer than himself.

"Not a clue," Sawyer growled. He threaded across three lanes of traffic and snapped on his right signal. "But she won't be able to say no to a diamond." He pulled into the parking lot of a chain jewelry store. "Wish I knew what kind to get."

Adam chuckled. "I can help with that. Riley had a comment for every ring she saw before picking the one she wanted." Maybe he could find a Christmas gift for Riley while he was in there.

"I can't believe you're fake-engaged."

It had felt kind of good to let someone in on his secret. Adam trusted Sawyer not to spill the beans, even though Noah shod horses regularly in Saddle Springs. The Delgado family hired a different farrier, though.

"Fake-engaged is kind of fun. Lots of side benefits."

Sawyer looked at him sharply. "I thought—"

"Not *that*, dude. I'm not falling into your trap. Too much emotional stuff hitches a ride with sex." He should know. "Kissing is my limit these days. And she's darn good at it."

"Just marry her."

Adam laughed. "Nah, that's not our deal." He'd had a week or two daydreaming about it, but then Riley had turned a cold shoulder, and that was that. He shoved the car door open. "Let's go find your Anna a ring she can't resist."

But it took more than a ring. Adam knew that much.

WHY HAD Riley agreed to Dakota's invitation again? Because here she was on a Thursday evening in a Jewel Lake townhouse with a woman and a little boy she barely knew.

But Dakota had made the trip to Rockstead to pick her up, and with Adam off in Texas, the ranch seemed quiet and lonely. Kathryn wanted to fill Riley's evenings, but that was a bad idea. It seemed only planning a wedding kept Adam's mom from teetering back into full depression, and Riley didn't want to be responsible for offering even more false hope and adding to the issues.

"See Woody?" Toby thrust a cowboy action figure in Riley's face.

"You like Toy Story?"

The little guy nodded enthusiastically and charged down the short hallway.

Dakota laughed. "If you go in his room, prepare to be overwhelmed. There's more than one reason I didn't offer you his bedroom for tonight. Now, if you'd come on a weekend when he's up at the ranch, you could have decided for yourself."

"The sofa will be fine." Riley'd already had a peek, and the living room furniture looked thick and comfy. It was just for one night, after all. She could survive anything.

"I thought we'd go over to the Golden Grill for dinner. Is that okay? I cook as little as I can get by with, and Toby loves their nuggets and fries."

"That sounds fine. They have great food." She'd only ever eaten there with Adam, but it was their usual Sunday lunch spot. Half the crowd from Creekside Fellowship reconvened at the diner after the benediction. "Where do you work?"

Dakota flipped her hair over her shoulder. "I manage the western wear shop downtown."

"Ooh, I could use some new duds."

"I took tomorrow off, but we could stop by for a bit if you like."

What else would they do all day? "Sure. And you need to show me all the sights of Jewel Lake. I haven't seen much of the town, and I have all my Christmas shopping to do." What on earth was she going to get Adam?

"Toby!" called Dakota. "Time to go to the Golden Grill."

"Coming, Mama." The little guy careened around the corner and into Dakota's arms.

A woman who scooped her giggling son and twirled him around couldn't be a bad person, could she? Riley'd seen Toby soak up ranch life, but it was obvious this was his real home. Mind you, it would be hard for anyone to relax around Travis. He was just as driven as his father. Maybe Dakota would confide in her...

Bad idea, because girl-talk went both ways, and Riley had nothing to share. Nothing from New Mexico, and definitely nothing about her relationship with Adam.

Toby tugged on his little cowboy boots, and they headed out the door.

A few minutes later, Riley had a plate of chicken-fried steak and mashed potatoes doused in thick brown gravy in front of her. Across the booth, Dakota's gaze swung between Riley's plate and her own Caesar Chicken Salad. Was Riley supposed to be embarrassed by her appetite? She worked hard at a physical job. She'd burn those calories, no problem. Besides, Dakota might be a little taller, but Riley'd bet they wore the same size clothes. She'd go ahead and enjoy her dinner, thanks.

A shadow fell over the table, and she glanced up. Scotty. Her heart seized.

"Mind if I join you?"

Riley tried to get a refusal out, but Dakota beat her to words. "Sure. Make room, would you, Riley? You've met my brother, Scott."

"Unca Scotty!"

"Hey, buddy." Scotty's gaze swiveled back to Riley, his eyebrows raised.

Did she dare make a scene? Not in this diner, where she had once before. Besides, she wasn't beholden to Scotty anymore. Jewel Lake wasn't an unknown blip on the map like when she'd arrived in his truck two months back. There was nothing to fear.

That didn't mean she wanted him next to her, but she scooted over reluctantly.

Something flashed in his eyes — triumph, maybe — at her movement. "Where's Cavanagh?"

Riley didn't want him to know Adam was far away.

"Texas," supplied Dakota. "It was a friend's funeral, wasn't it, Riley?"

"Yes."

Scotty sidled closer on the bench seat. "How long is he gone for?"

"He'll be back tomorrow. That's how I got to borrow Riley for overnight."

"Is that so?" It might be his sister that answered every question, but his gaze was all for Riley.

Her chin came up and she placed both hands flat on the table. "Perhaps you've forgotten Adam and I are engaged?" Her diamond gleamed in the light above the booth.

"Are you now?" A glint of amusement shone in his eyes.

"Definitely. We're planning a spring wedding."

Dakota squealed. "Have you set a date yet?"

"Not yet."

"I hope I get an invitation." Scotty's voice was low and intimate. "After all, I believe I had something to do with this... incident."

Riley's gaze flew to his mocking face. How much had he guessed? Because the only proof she had was a diamond ring and the fact she'd lived at Rockstead ever since that night.

He winked at her.

Her gut quaked. Maybe chicken-fried steak wasn't the best idea, after all.

Scotty waved down a server and ordered a large coke and a double bacon cheeseburger with fries.

Riley could endure this if she had to, and she wasn't going to let him know how much he rattled her. That meant she'd have to make major inroads on her dinner. Somehow she'd survive the Golden Grill. Scotty'd better not insert himself into Dakota's townhouse afterward. She'd put her foot down at that, for sure.

A group of people entered the diner, laughing and talking as the host led them to the table next to where Riley sat with the Ericksons. A burly man lifted a furry coat from the shoulders of an older woman, and Riley froze in recognition.

Mrs. McDiarmid's eyes met Riley's. Then the church

secretary's gaze took in Dakota, Toby, and Scotty, and her eyebrows lifted slightly.

Scotty's proximity did not look good. It didn't take a genius to figure that out.

The couple with their backs to the booth glanced behind them. Pastor Marshall Smith and his wife.

Riley smiled and waved before turning to Toby. "What's your favorite movie?" she asked the little guy.

Dakota groaned as Toby's eyes lit up.

CHAPTER EIGHTEEN

"Didja miss me?" Adam tucked Riley close against him in the foyer to the main house. The past week had been surreal. All he wanted was to go back to the time before the trip to Texas, before running into Erickson at Running Creek, before fall had turned into winter. A doozy of a snowstorm had greeted him and Sawyer this afternoon upon their arrival at the Missoula airport and made his drive up the ranch road more than a little entertaining.

Emma giggled.

That's what he got for finally catching up to Riley minutes after the dinner gong at five o'clock. At least she wouldn't outright avoid him in front of his family. He lowered his head to kiss her.

Alexia laughed. "She missed you so much she went to Jewel Lake and spent the night with Dakota."

Adam pulled back and looked into Riley's guilty eyes. But why guilty? "You and Dakota are friends now?"

She averted her gaze. "Sort of."

What were sort-of friends? Maybe he didn't want to know.

"I had some Christmas shopping to do." She still didn't look at him.

Good thing he'd taken advantage of Sawyer's lengthy perusal of the jewelry store to pick out a gift for Riley. They didn't do much for Christmas around Rockstead — Declan figured the holiday was only a front for materialism and a way to shirk work — but Riley probably expected something, even though the undecorated house had likely muted any anticipation.

Just then Blake and Travis entered with Toby, who broke free and ran over to hug Riley's leg. She grinned down at the little guy and squeezed his shoulder before he darted back to Travis's side.

Huh. That was new. Toby rarely bothered with anyone at the ranch besides Emma and Alexia.

Travis narrowed his gaze and looked between Riley and Adam. Was Adam supposed to know what was going on? Because he didn't.

"You guys coming in for dinner or what?" hollered Ryder from the dining room.

Adam rested his hand on the small of Riley's back and escorted her to her place.

Another surprise. Mom sat at the foot of the table. She smiled between him and Riley. "Welcome home, son."

"It's good to be here." He meant it, too. He clasped Riley's hand in his after they'd settled into their chairs. Declan nodded at him, and Adam wondered who said grace when he wasn't home. He kept it short, though he had a lot to be thankful for today. Going to a friend's funeral did that to a guy.

Hanging out with another friend whose pregnant ex-girlfriend wanted nothing to do with him was another reminder. He'd told Sawyer he had no expectations about him and Riley making their fake commitment real, but that wasn't completely true. What he didn't know was what to do about it since Riley had cooled off considerably the last few days before Adam had flown to Texas. Something to do with running into Scotty Erickson at Running Creek, but what? Adam was missing a clue or two. Nothing new there when it came to women.

When the meal had been consumed and the remains of dessert cleared away, Mom cleared her throat. Adam looked at her in surprise. She rarely had anything to say in front of Declan or his boys.

"Sunday is Christmas Eve. We'll be gathering after lunch in the family room downstairs. The girls have a surprise for all their brothers. Then we'll be heading into Jewel Lake for the Christmas Eve service at Creekside Fellowship." She looked straight down the table at her husband. "I'd appreciate it if everyone attended."

Whoa, she was tackling Declan? *Way to grow a backbone, Mom!*

Everyone at the table froze, heads swiveling between them as Declan stared back at his wife.

"I sing manger song," announced Toby into the perfect stillness.

"We wouldn't want to miss that," Mom said with a smile. "Would we, Grandpa?"

Declan's jaw twitched. He shot a look around the table.

Pleading for a diversion, maybe? But no one offered it. Finally, he gave a terse nod. "We could do that, I guess."

"That's settled then." Mom folded her napkin, rose, and turned from the table. "Thank you, Cook." She swept from the room.

The only thing that kept Adam grounded was Riley's hand in his as he pulled to his feet. He didn't dare meet anyone's gaze, not his brothers', not his stepbrothers', and definitely not Declan's. He held his breath as he helped Riley into her down parka and didn't release it until the door closed behind them.

"Wow," he breathed.

"What just happened?"

"A few things." Snow whipped sideways as they descended the porch steps. Adam kept a firm grip on Riley's hand. "One, my mother never challenges Declan in front of us boys. Like, absolutely never. I honestly can't remember if it's ever happened before."

"What else?"

"And Declan agreed to go to church. Yeah, she kind of cornered him, but he could have said no. I have no idea why he didn't."

"Because of Toby?"

"I guess so, but remember he isn't my mom's grandkid. She has very little to do with Travis or Toby. Hardly any more with Blake or Ryder." Adam pondered it some more while they walked down the lane toward the cabins.

"I was beginning to wonder if your family had something against Christmas, to be honest. There's like no decorations or anything."

"Declan's not into it." Adam's mouth twisted. "My

parents sure were. Dad could hardly keep a surprise for even a day or two. He always went shopping for Mom on Christmas Eve so he wouldn't have to keep the secret for as long."

"Aw, that's sweet." Riley's fingers squeezed his. "You still miss your dad, don't you?"

"Yeah. A lot. Even though it's been over fifteen years." Time to change the subject. "What does your family usually do for Christmas?"

Riley laughed sharply. "Parties."

ADAM COULDN'T KNOW how his sudden question pierced her with memories. Everything with her mom and dad had always been about putting on a front. The biggest tree. The most stylish decorations. The biggest party with the season's most vaunted caterer and musicians.

Certainly nothing as cozy as the Cavanagh afternoon promised to be, and very little about Adam's family oozed pleasantries. Still, everyone would be there, and Riley couldn't imagine Declan and Kathryn yelling obscenities at each other in front of their kids, then covering it up with saccharine sweet smiles as their guests arrived.

Oh, she was under no delusions about the status of the Cavanaghs' marriage. Bedrooms on different levels of the mansion told that story loud and clear. But she could handle chilly. It was a lot less threatening to everyone around them than the way her parents did things.

"Will you get a chance to see your sister? She lives in

Missoula, right? We could drive in one afternoon if you like. At least once the storm is over."

"I don't think Jodie wants to see me."

Adam's arm slid around her shoulders. "You sure?"

"She's all wrapped up in that guy she's living with. We had a fight about it."

"I'm sorry to hear."

Adam somehow seemed different since returning from Texas. The moodiness from that day at Running Creek was gone. Even the cockiness of the cowboy she'd kind of fallen for over the past two months was gone. This Adam was gentler. More genuine.

Too bad it didn't change anything in the long run.

"You haven't told me much about your parents. Are they together?"

"There's not much to say about them."

Adam chuckled. "Sorry, I don't believe you. Your dad's a State Senator? You must have a ton of stories."

Riley pulled away from Adam's arm. "I don't remember telling you that."

"What's the big deal? Everyone has a job. My stepdad's a rancher. Your dad's a Sen—"

"There are a lot of Dunnings in the US."

He frowned, but his eyebrows rose. "True. Did I get the wrong one? Because New Mexico State Senator Dunning has two daughters, and one of them is named Riley."

If he'd figured that out, Raul was likely to come out of the woodwork next. All those photos in the papers… yikes. She managed to keep her voice even. "No biggie."

"I don't understand you, Ry. Why would you want to keep it a secret what your dad does? I mean, I get that politics is a volatile topic and both sides hate the other, but New Mexico is a long way from Montana. And, I'm guessing, most people get into politics because they care about people's rights." Adam shrugged. "I wouldn't know for sure, because I've never given running for office a passing thought."

Riley couldn't speak for other politicians, but Dad's venture into the arena had very little to do with the concerns of the average citizen. And then there was Raul. "Can we drop the subject?"

"We could, but it sounds like you need someone to talk to. Here I am."

"I don't need someone to talk to. The less said about my father, the better."

"Don't you want your parents at your wedding? Your father should walk you down the aisle."

Riley whirled toward Adam and parked her hands on her hips. "Have you forgotten there won't be a wedding?"

"Shh." He glanced around.

She heaved a sigh. "Adam, seriously. We need to get everything taken care of soon. This is driving me crazy." *He* was driving her crazy. Sure, if they were really going to get married, he deserved to know all about the ugly situation in Santa Fe she'd run from. But they weren't. "You need to talk to Declan and move things forward. I'm getting pressured from every angle. I ran into Mrs. McDiarmid in Jewel Lake last night, and she was pressing me for a date for the church." While the church secretary glowered at Scotty Erickson sitting far too close to Riley, but Adam didn't need to know that.

"We agreed on three months. It's only been two."

"Adam, I need out."

"We shouldn't be having this conversation outside."

"We don't need to have a conversation at all. Just *do* something. I need out of here by the end of the year. Make it happen." She whirled away and marched toward her cabin. Was it her imagination, or was there a crunch of a boot in snow from a direction that was not Adam?

Probably her overactive imagination. Whatever. If someone was there, eavesdropping, Adam could take care of any explanations. The cowboy could lie like nobody's business.

ADAM TOOK a few steps toward cabin six and nearly rammed directly into someone. His heart jolted until he realized it was Nathaniel. Then it pounded some more. This was not information he wanted his brother to know.

Nathaniel glowered at him. "What was all that about?"

"What was all *what* about?" Adam kept his voice even.

"You know." Nat thumbed toward Riley's cabin, where the door closed firmly behind her, taking the brief rectangle of light with it.

"Whatever you think you heard wasn't the whole story." Adam shoved his shoulder against his brother's in an effort to get past.

Nathaniel blocked him. "It never is. Want to talk?"

"Not really."

"I think you do."

Adam pivoted and stared his brother in the eye. "Is that some kind of threat?"

"If the boot fits, wear it." Nathaniel's stance did not soften, nor did the hardness in his gaze.

At least it was Nathaniel who'd overheard, not Travis or — shudder — Declan. Nat would understand that everything Adam did was for all three of the Anderson brothers. It would be okay.

Adam sighed. "Come in then."

"Darn right." Nathaniel fell into step beside Adam and followed him into the cabin, where they both shucked their winter coats and snow-covered boots.

Adam gave a thought to the warmth in Texas he'd experienced only this morning as he tossed a couple of logs into the wood stove. He turned, hoping his brother would have disappeared. No such luck.

Nathaniel stood in front of the door, feet planted and arms crossed in front of him. "I knew there was something fishy about you and Riley. What's in it for her?"

"You don't understand."

"Darn right I don't. Educate me." Nat held up a hand. "Wait. Don't. This is all about Running Creek, isn't it?"

"It should belong to us. To you and Noah and me."

Nathaniel removed his hat long enough to shove his hand through his hair as he shook his head. "Ever heard of just being up front? If Declan finds out what you've done, our chance will be gone." His hand chopped through the air.

"He won't find out." Adam stared his brother in the eye. "Unless you tell him."

"Look. Here's what I don't get. You're lying to everyone, including me. But, at the same time, you're pretending to be this good little Christian boy, like you had some kind of experience that makes you better than the rest of us."

Adam winced as his brother's words sliced through him. How had he managed to justify all this in his own head? Because Nathaniel was right.

He'd blown it.

CHAPTER NINETEEN

This would be the Sunday Riley wished she could feign illness and stay locked up in her little cabin, or, better yet, be somewhere far away from western Montana. Definitely not New Mexico, though.

Ugh. How had she made such a big mess of her life? Raul was in her rearview mirror. Adam soon would be, and the thought she could live in nearby Jewel Lake after their breakup was so laughably ridiculous, she should be collapsed in giggles.

Definitely not how she felt as she strolled into church on Sunday morning, hand-in-hand with Adam. If only she could halfway match his nonchalance and his smiles for everyone around them as though nothing was wrong.

Everything was wrong. She'd gone and fallen for Adam even with all her best defenses in place. Feeling his warm palm against hers with their fingers entwined made her want so much more, but it was all about the ranch for him.

For Raul, it had only been about getting close to her

dad. About his own political aspirations. She'd been nothing but a tool, and she'd been totally clueless.

This time she'd walked in with her eyes wide open, or so she'd thought. Falling in love with this conniving cowboy had not been part of the plan. He'd kept to his part, but it needed to end.

Where would she go after New Year's? She'd meant the ultimatum she'd given Adam. One more week and she was out of here, regardless of whether he'd secured Running Creek or not. If she had to do without the ten grand, so be it. She was done. She had her wages tucked in the bank in Jewel Lake, so she was in better shape than in October.

One more week to survive. Now she endured the Christmas Eve morning service with the carols and the sermon of hope and joy that did nothing to penetrate the dullness in her soul.

She loved Christmas. She did. Or at least, she used to, but recent years had soured her. This was one for the history books.

Your own fault, Riley. Instead of confronting Dad and Raul, you ran. You hitchhiked with jerks like Scotty Erickson. You threw yourself at a total stranger in the diner lobby. You agreed to his preposterous terms. You deserve every bit of unhappiness you've achieved.

As the interminable service came to an end, Mrs. McDiarmid turned from in front of them, her gaze flitting between Riley and Adam. "Oh, it's good to see you together. I thought..."

Adam's fingers found Riley's as he smiled at the church secretary. "You thought what?"

"Well, Riley and Sco... never mind." Her face reddened as she grabbed her purse and edged out of the aisle.

Riley felt Adam's gaze but didn't look up at him. "Oh, look. There's Lyssa Quinn. Do you know her? She teaches third grade at Creekside Academy."

"How do you know her?"

"Um, she lives next door to Dakota. We met on the doorstep the other night."

"Where was Scotty?" Adam's voice was low.

"Not there." Riley's brain shot in a hundred directions. "We just watched a movie at Dakota's place after she tucked Toby in bed. A rom com. The new one with Meg Ryan." She was babbling, but she couldn't seem to stop.

Kathryn and the twins edged out the other end of the aisle, and the crowd around them thinned.

"Where was Scotty?" Adam's voice was even quieter, but the steel in it was unmistakable.

"He invited himself to our table at the diner. I didn't encourage him, no matter what you think." Just the thought. The guy made her skin crawl.

"And the McDiarmids were there, too?"

Riley nodded, daring a quick peek at Adam's face from beneath her lashes. Oh, boy. His jaw firmed, and his eyes were hard and unyielding. "I couldn't help it." How weak her voice sounded.

"Have you been sneaking around with him behind my back?"

Riley snatched her hand out of his and crossed her arms over her chest. "Are you kidding me? First of all, he's a creep. And secondly, this is the first time I've been off the ranch without you for two solid months."

"And straight into Erickson's arms."

"Are you being stupid on purpose?" she hissed.

"What am I supposed to think?"

"You're supposed to believe me. Trust me." *Love me. Marry me.*

Adam bent slightly so she couldn't avoid his piercing eyes. "You know the problem with our charade? I don't know where it begins or ends, but I do know you made a promise."

Her chin tipped up. "I've kept it."

"You'd better have, because if Mrs. McDiarmid gets back to Declan, this gig is up."

"One week. It's up to you to nail things down before she does that. Anyway, when are they ever going to see each other?"

"Have you forgotten? He's coming to church tonight."

In the heat of the moment, she *hadn't* remembered. "Oh. Right."

"I'm warning you, Riley. It's on your head if this falls apart."

"Not a chance, cowboy. I've put my life on hold for you. I've done everything you asked me to do. Have you even talked to Declan after that one time?"

His jaw tensed. "The timing hasn't been right."

"It better be right any minute now, is all I can say. I'm tired of living a lie."

"You two coming?"

Riley whirled to see Nathaniel at the end of the aisle, his face as blank as his brother's. Adam had said Nat had overheard too much on Friday. It was clear whose side he was on. As it should be, she supposed. The lines were clearly drawn. Soon everyone in this disjointed family would be against her, and she'd deserve every bit of their scorn.

"We're coming." Adam's pressure on Riley's lower back wasn't as gentle or tender as usual. His sharp knuckle dug hard as she gritted her teeth and moved in the direction she was being pushed.

"You coming for lunch at the Golden Grill?" asked Nathaniel.

"No," said Riley just as Adam answered, "Of course."

Sure, it was their habit, but it was Christmas Eve. Weren't they due back at Rockstead soon? Not only that, she didn't want to keep up the pretense in a public place.

One more week. Then she'd fly to a... a beach in Florida, maybe, where she could cry in peace.

NOAH, Blake, and Ryder carried the conversation over lunch at the Golden Grill. Just as well. Adam was still reeling. His house of cards wobbled over his head. If he were honest with himself, a few cards had already slipped off the edifice.

Back at Rockstead, Mom and the twins had decorated the family room downstairs with a fake tree and a few handmade decorations. A small pile of gifts sat beneath it.

Declan took his place in a large recliner across the room, his face set in stone. The brothers gathered around on the sectional and chairs. Toby ran circles with Ezra on the fluffy white rug until he collapsed in Travis's lap, the Yorkie panting at their feet.

Adam wrapped his arm around Riley's shoulders on the love seat and pulled her close. She leaned against him just enough that no one probably noticed the tension in her body, but he could feel it. What had seemed like such a good idea that October night had turned out to be anything but.

Emma and Alexia proudly presented each brother with a framed watercolor painting. Riley opened one that matched Adam's — two presentations of the autumn woods with glacier-clad peaks in the distance. "For your new home," Emma offered shyly.

"Thanks." Riley jumped to her feet and hugged each twin. "I'll treasure this always."

If anyone noticed she hadn't included Adam, no one reacted. When she sat back down, she left a little room between them and reached behind herself for a package. "Merry Christmas, cowboy." She presented it to Adam with a smile that didn't quite reach her eyes.

He tore the wrap away, aware that all eyes were on them, and revealed a black shirt with a horse's head embroidered in gray tones. He leaned over and pecked her lips. "Thanks. It's great."

"I'm glad you like it."

"I have something for you, too." Adam tugged a small gift-wrapped box from his shirt pocket.

Riley gave him a questioning look as she slipped the ribbon from around the box. Inside lay a diamond necklace with matching earrings. She bit her lip and touched the gleaming jewelry. "It's beautiful, Adam. Thank you."

"Oh, that will be lovely with your wedding dress!" Mom

exclaimed from her spot beside the tree. "Have you picked a style yet?"

"Not yet." Riley didn't look up.

"Let me put the necklace on you." Adam lifted the dainty chain from the box while Riley swept her unruly hair to one side. Then he slid it around her neck and fastened the tiny clasp. He couldn't resist pressing a kiss to her bare skin.

"Enough mush." Travis's disgusted voice broke the moment.

The girls giggled, and Toby echoed them.

After the way the last few days had gone, Riley was probably counting up the dollar value of the jewelry. He'd had such high hopes in Amarillo, as though Sawyer's optimism had rubbed off on him. Still, an extravagant gift was necessary for show.

Several more presents were exchanged. The Cavanaghs had never been big on it, so it wasn't a major deal.

At least, until Declan cleared his throat, and his sharp gaze landed on Adam.

"Your mother and I have been talking."

Adam tried to swallow. Failed. Riley's fingers laced with his, and he drew strength from the touch.

"Noah, Nathaniel, this pertains to you as well."

His twin brothers exchanged a look. The other brothers also glanced between themselves.

"I'd like to..." Declan paused, and his gaze bounced off Mom. So, this was *her* wording, not his. "*We'd* like to offer Running Creek Ranch back to you boys. I'll be honest. I've been waiting to see some signs of maturity."

Adam felt heat creep up his face. If only his stepfather knew.

"Until recently, only one of you showed any signs of growing up. Congratulations on establishing your farrier business, Noah. You have a good reputation. You've done me proud."

"Thank you, sir."

Adam was pretty sure this was the first time their stepfather had ever acknowledged any of them for a job well done.

Declan looked at Nathaniel and shook his head. "I'm still waiting for a sign you have any ambition of any sort, but your mother insists that two out of three is enough. And with you, Adam, engaged to be married and taking on solid responsibility around here, she might be right."

"Breathe," whispered Riley, nudging his ribs.

Adam inhaled, his gaze still fixed on his stepfather.

"What day is the wedding again?"

"We, uh..." Adam stuttered. "We haven't decided, exactly."

Declan's eyebrows rose. "Why's that?"

Adam had no answer. The question made sense, though. Surely any normal engaged couple would have made this decision long ago.

"I'm not sure when my parents can come all the way up here," Riley said, squeezing his hand. "That's part of the holdup."

"Here's what we're going to do." Declan looked over at Mom, then at the twins, and finally, again, at Adam and Riley. "After the wedding, we'll sign the papers for the ranch. How you boys divide things is up to you. Figure out who's going to live in the house and how the others will be compensated." He shrugged. "Or keep living in the cabins here and ride for Rockstead. Up to you."

Somewhere in the middle of that, Adam's brain had caught on the timing. "*After* the wedding, sir?"

His stepfather's gaze skewered his. "That's what I said. Please note I'll need at least sixty days to remove the current tenants, so there's no point in eloping next week. All the paperwork could be completed by the first of March at the earliest."

After the wedding. And Riley wanted to break up and leave by the end of the year. She'd drawn the line in the snow — no way would she stick around long enough to marry him.

Oh… and then divorce him.

Adam had lost. He'd lost everything, right on the heels of gaining it, only no one knew except him and Riley and Nathaniel. He opened his mouth, but what could he say? Call off the farce now? When would he ever get the chance to regain control of Running Creek for him and his brothers if he let this opportunity slip away?

He turned to Riley, pouring all his desperate hope into his gaze. "What do you say, honey? Early March?"

Something like sympathy lurked in her eyes. "I'll get back to you on that, cowboy."

CHAPTER TWENTY

So near, yet so far.

Riley stared into the swath of light in the darkness caused by the beams from Adam's truck headlights. If only she could see the way clear in front of her life even this much. She'd been holding it together since Declan's announcement a couple of hours ago, and she'd do the same at the Christmas Eve service at Creekside Fellowship. But now, during the drive to Jewel Lake, when she could say whatever she wanted without fear of being overheard, she didn't even know where to start.

Across the cab, Adam's gloved hands flexed on the steering wheel. The set of his jaw and his unwavering focus had nothing to do with slippery road conditions or the possibility of wildlife. No, she was certain it had everything to do with his stepfather's words.

When he was still silent as they crossed the last cattle-guard before the highway, Riley couldn't stand it anymore. "What now?"

"I've lost." His voice was flat, devoid of emotion. "Declan will never give me a second chance at Running Creek. I'll never measure up. Not after this."

"How can you just give up? Your dad's ranch is your dream."

"What, you want to get married then divorced after the papers have been signed? I doubt it. You want out of here next week."

"Marriage isn't something to be taken lightly." Famous last words from someone who'd glibly agreed to take engagement lightly. She'd never dreamed it would come to this, though.

Adam sighed. "I agree. I can't ask that of you. In this day and age, the whole thing is ridiculous, anyway. Nearly every couple I know is living together. Declan's not even a Christian. What does he care if we get married?"

"He married your mother."

"Yeah. Why?"

Riley shook her head. How should she know? Kathryn mostly avoided her husband, but occasionally she proved she had a backbone. Like over getting the family together this afternoon. At first Riley had thought it was because of Toby — Travis would be handing his son over to Dakota at the Christmas Eve service shortly. But now she wondered if Kathryn had orchestrated the whole thing to give Declan a platform for making his announcement to Adam and his brothers.

If it was supposed to be some kind of Christmas or wedding gift, it had fallen very, very flat.

"What are you going to do?"

"I don't know. I'm done with rodeo after Ace. I've got some savings, but not enough to buy my own ranch."

And he'd be ten grand poorer when he paid her off. He still would, even though their ruse had fallen short, wouldn't he?

He shrugged. "Maybe I can hire on at the Delgados' ranch over near Saddle Springs. Sawyer's a good buddy, and his love life is as pathetic as mine."

That stung. "I thought he was trying to win over the mother of his baby."

"He is. Or at least, he was. But she left Eaglecrest while he and I were in Texas, and he doesn't know where she is. Clearly, she wants nothing to do with him."

"Oh, no. That's too bad." Riley's heart went out to the pregnant woman. She must be so troubled. So confused.

They passed the overlook and began the descent into Jewel Lake. He glanced over at Riley. "How about you? Got any plans?"

The nonchalant way he uttered the words pounded another nail in the coffin of Riley's dreams. "Nothing for sure."

"Going back to New Mexico?"

"No." She wrapped her arms around her middle and watched the businesses at the edge of Jewel Lake roll by. "My parents have a sham of a marriage, too." Now, why had she confided that?

He responded with a humorless grunt. "Seems to be all the rage in the parental generation. I don't want that."

There was an option. A viable option. She bit her tongue. "Me, neither. When I marry, it will be for love. Because I can't live without him."

"Not with planning to get a divorce a week later?"

"No."

He sighed as he turned onto Agate Street along Creekside Park. "Can't say that I blame you. It's just hard to let my dream go, you know? It's been my only goal for fifteen years."

The words were on the tip of her tongue. *Marry me for real, Adam.* But if he didn't even consider it a possibility, she couldn't throw herself at him. Been there, done that, got the engagement ring and all the fake promises a girl could want. No, he'd been decisive that night. He knew what he wanted and had figured out a way to get it.

If only he'd be as decisive now.

He turned into the church parking lot, found a spot, and cut the engine before turning to look at her. "Ready?"

"Sure." But she'd never felt less Christmassy in her life.

It might be Christmas morning, but thankfully the family had done all their celebrating, such as it had been, yesterday. Cook had taken a couple of days off, so Adam didn't bother going over to the main house for breakfast. He filled his thermos with coffee from his French press, shoved a handful of protein bars into his parka pocket, and headed out to the stable to saddle up Jupiter. What he needed was a day with just him, God, and a horse out in nature. So what if it was ten below? He wasn't a sissy.

Only the whiffle of Jupiter's breath and the creak of the saddle kept absolute silence at bay. The trail along the tree-lined creek lay in snowy shadow but, in the distance, sunlight gleamed on glacier-clad peaks. If only he could get there, but too many obstacles lay between. Hills, valleys, cliffs, river crossings, mountain lions... the list went on and on. Insurmountable.

Sort of like his life. He could see happiness from here, but there was no path. The trail he'd blazed ended on the edge of a precipice, and his only option was to retreat and embark on a massive detour. A route that would end in a different destination. Maybe it would be an okay place. Maybe he'd be somewhat satisfied, but it wasn't what he really wanted.

He could throw himself on Declan's mercy, but the man had none. If his stepfather found out Adam had been lying to him for over two months, Running Creek Ranch would be forever out of reach. But it wasn't *if*. It was *when*. Unless he and Riley just broke up now and he kept pretending it had been real.

Adam couldn't do that. He was tired of deception.

So am I.

He looked around, but no one was near. The snow was unmarred in every direction but the one he'd come. Yet the voice had been clear.

The voice had been God's.

Adam stared down at his gloved hands holding Jupiter's reins. A shift in his weight. A slight movement of the reins. A soft word. Any of those were enough to signal a change to his steadfast mount. Jupiter was superbly trained. He did Adam's bidding at the first indication.

Once Adam had heard God's voice clearly. Months ago,

before Ace's accident. He and his friends had vowed to turn their backs on the life they'd been living and follow God. Now Ace was dead. Sawyer's ex had gone missing with their unborn child. And Adam's dream had drifted away like Jupiter's breath in the frosty air.

Instead of trusting God to open his path, Adam had grabbed the first opportunity to take matters into his own hands. Look where that had gotten him.

"God, I screwed up big time."

Jupiter twitched his ears and sighed.

Even the faithful gelding was against him, but Adam wouldn't let that hold him back. "I'm sorry, Lord. I don't know what to do. What I've done will affect my mom. My brothers. Riley... I've hurt her. Demanded my own way at all cost. I've been so selfish."

But Running Creek was his legacy. How could a woman in labor suffer more in birth than he agonized over this death of a dream? The pain was real. Gut-twisting.

"For I know the plans I have for you," declares the Lord, "plans to prosper you and not to harm you, plans to give you hope and a future."

Adam had known that verse since he was a kid in Sunday school. Why hadn't he trusted it, especially when he'd decided to follow Jesus once again?

A hope and a future.

God wasn't out to get him. Adam had barely given God a chance to reveal His plan. And now that hope-and-prosper path was gone through Adam's own stupidity.

"I'm so sorry."

But was he repentant because he was in a corner, or

because he'd done wrong? His conscience had been biting him for a while, but he'd been muzzling it. Shoving it aside. The ends would justify the means.

Only... they didn't.

And his dream had materialized before his eyes but had proven to be only a mirage. He'd lived a lie. He'd convinced Riley to live a lie. And all he'd have to show for it would be his stepfather's scorn and the bitterness of Noah and Nathaniel's reproach. And his mother...

He didn't want to think of what his actions would do to Mom. How Emma and Alexia would stop looking up to him.

"God, what do I do now? I'm sorry. I'm really, truly sorry. I didn't think beyond Running Creek. Much as I love that place, it's only real estate. It's not worth losing respect. It's not worth wrecking my relationship with You. Please, please forgive me."

If we confess our sins, he is faithful and just and will forgive us our sins and purify us from all unrighteousness.

That was in First John somewhere. It didn't say only some kinds of sin. It said *all* unrighteousness. That had to cover Adam's lies, right?

He nudged Jupiter up the bank toward the meadow. Field grasses and wildflowers lay blanketed beneath a palette of snow, fresh and clean.

Wasn't there something in the Bible about sins, red like scarlet, becoming white as snow?

Adam reined Jupiter in and stared at the unmarred surface in front of him. The sun angled over the trees now, pouring its bright white light across the snow. The meadow dazzled like a diamond mine. Like the jewelry he'd given Riley for Christmas... on steroids.

There was no out-giving God.

What was he going to do?

What could he do?

He had to confess his sin to his stepfather and set Riley free. Oh, how he was going to miss her when she was gone. He'd gotten so used to having her around Rockstead, to riding out with her, to playing cards with her. To kissing her as though he had a right.

It didn't matter anymore that she'd started it.

He'd immediately kicked it to the next level and kept it there.

It didn't matter anymore that she'd gone along.

Adam was the man. He was responsible to lead her to a closer walk with Jesus, not to encourage her to lie more convincingly every day.

Shame surged through his veins at what he'd become, all because he'd let his desire for his dad's ranch overwhelm his good sense. He hadn't prayed. Not really. He'd figured a resourceful guy could manage this on his own.

Showed how smart he was. Not very. He'd do better now. He'd spend some time seeking God and then head back.

A few hours later, he unsaddled Jupiter and reached for the curry comb. He looked up at the thudding of footsteps on the stone alley, but instead of Riley, the twins appeared.

Emma climbed up on the gate. "Where were you?"

"Riding."

Alexia leaned against the gate, her arms crossed on the

top rail, and rolled her eyes. "We looked everywhere for you."

"Oh?" Adam kept the comb moving rhythmically down Jupiter's flank.

"Riley had to go to Santa Fe," Emma informed him. "Nathaniel drove her to the airport in Missoula, since you weren't here."

He froze, slowly raising his head to look at the twins. "What are you talking about?" Just last night she'd told him New Mexico was the last place she'd go. Now she up and went with only a moment's notice? Didn't add up.

Alexia shook her head. "Her dad was in a bad accident. They're not sure if he's going to make it."

"No way." How suddenly things changed.

"Yes way."

"She couldn't wait for me? I'd have gone with her."

"You could call her. I don't know what time her flight is. Do they even fly on Christmas Day?"

All those dazzling snow diamonds had moved in and frozen his gut solid. He'd been off feeling sorry for himself while Riley'd had to deal with news like that all on her own?

No. He'd needed the ride. Needed the clarity, the time of repentance and prayer. But he'd failed Riley for the millionth time. "Did she leave me a note or anything?" She must have. She wouldn't just leave without saying goodbye. Or would she decide this was the best way to break things off?

Alexia shrugged. "She went into your cabin before she left. She was probably looking for you."

"Adam?" Emma's eyes were wide. "Riley's coming back, isn't she?"

"Of cour—" But he couldn't say that with certainty. "I'll have to call her and see what's going on." He held up the curry comb. "Who wants to earn ten bucks to finish up with Jupiter?"

The twins looked at each other. Emma slid off the gate. "Ten for each of us, and you have a deal."

CHAPTER TWENTY-ONE

Riley settled into the narrow airplane seat beside her sister. If she'd thought things couldn't get more uncomfortable than the chilly drive to Missoula refusing to answer Nathaniel's accusations, she hadn't counted on her weepy sister.

Jodie pressed a sodden tissue to her blotchy face. "I can't believe Dad might d-die."

"I know." Riley clamped down on her emotions. One of them out of control was enough.

"Do you think he'll be okay?"

The report had sounded cautiously optimistic, but Riley knew nothing Jodie didn't. Dad's car had been T-boned by an SUV with a front-mounted winch that had crashed through the driver-side window, causing a spinal injury that might spell permanent paralysis... if he didn't die from his multitude of other injuries.

"I hope so." Riley couldn't think of much else to say. Regardless of her frustration at her parents' lifestyle and the way he'd stuck up for Raul in October, he was her dad.

The attendant began the pre-flight instructions, giving Riley a reprieve. Too bad this wasn't a direct flight. She wouldn't be able to feign sleep for the entire journey, but she'd do her best to turn Jodie's attention elsewhere.

"When's your wedding again?"

Elsewhere, but not there. Riley took a deep breath. She hadn't left any of her personal goods in her cabin. Would she return to Rockstead? It depended on Adam, but how much did she need to explain to Jodie?

She'd always tried to be a good role model for her sister. Mostly it had backfired. If Jodie found out what Riley had agreed to, she'd never look up to her again. Maybe that would be a relief.

Still, the confession stuck in Riley's throat. "I don't know. Adam and I had kind of a... a fight yesterday." Following the one the day before and the week before that. She rubbed her engagement ring. Should she have left it on his dresser when she'd entered to leave a note? He knew she'd planned to pawn it, so he wouldn't expect it back. But how could she part with it?

Jodie grabbed Riley's left hand as the plane began to pick up speed for takeoff. "That's quite a rock. He must love you a lot. A guy like that isn't going to let a little tiff get in the way."

"It wasn't that little. I don't see how we can get past it." How about if she took both his hands in hers and told him she actually truly loved him? He wouldn't believe her. He'd probably think she was just after security. After her share of Running Creek. Her heart sank. There was too much at stake.

"Want to talk about it?"

Did she? Holding it all in was twisting her guts tight, but no. "I have to process it first." And pray. She'd been ignoring God far too much, not really wanting His input.

Things were even more messed up, though. She and Adam started off on entirely the wrong foot, she'd fallen in love with him. She wasn't sure how it had happened or when, but it had.

He cared deeply. For his mom, for his brothers, for his family's legacy. He offered his stepfather the respect due to his position, even though he didn't actually like him.

He was a man of integrity. Yes, even with this major deviance, Riley knew she could trust him completely.

She turned to Jodie. "Tell me, how are things with Mick?"

"Why are we flying to Seattle before heading southeast?"

Riley raised her eyebrows. "Are you avoiding my question?"

"You dodged mine."

Fair enough. "If he's being a jerk, let me know, and I'll take him on. No one messes with people I love."

Jodie snorted. "Right. What're you going to do, kick his kneecaps?"

"I'll aim a little higher."

"If you're so tough, solve your own problems first."

Full circle, then. Out the tiny window, Riley watched the mountains below disappear amid gray clouds as the aircraft rose.

Returning to Santa Fe was the last thing she'd ever planned to do. Was Raul still in good standing with her dad? Would she be forced to see him? She'd only stay as long as it took to make sure Dad would survive, but where she'd go then, she had no idea.

Oh, Adam. Why hadn't they met in a different way?

ADAM REREAD Riley's note for the fourth time. It explained what she knew about her dad, but it said nothing about when — or if — she was coming back. Just a few terse words then her name signed with a heart over the i in place of the dot.

Alexia did that, too. Adam had noticed it on the painting she'd given him. It probably didn't mean anything, but it was all he had to cling to.

A rap sounded on his door. With his sisters grooming Jupiter and Nathaniel driving Riley, Adam could only hope it was Noah. But when he opened the door, he found his stepfather waiting on the stoop.

Adam took a deep breath and stepped back. "Come on in." Unformed prayers tumbled from his mind into the ether. *Please, God. Please help me.* Those were the only words he could form and repeat.

Declan stepped inside and closed the door behind him, his gaze never leaving Adam's face.

"Have a seat?"

"I don't think so. Tell me what is going on with Riley."

"I, uh..."

His stepfather crossed his arms as his eyebrows rose.

How much had Declan figured out? Was he guessing, or did he know something? "I doubt I know much more than you do." Adam lifted the note. "She's gone to be with her family."

"And you didn't go?"

"I didn't know before she left. I was out riding Jupiter. I, uh, had some thinking to do."

"Is she two-timing you with Scott Erickson? Because gossip came to my ears last night."

Adam let out a long breath. "There are rumors, but they aren't true. He refuses to leave her alone." This was the end of all Adam's dreams. Right here. He breathed another frantic prayer. "Truth is..." Oh, Lord, did he really have to go here?

Declan stared at him.

"I didn't think you'd let me have Running Creek if I couldn't prove to you I was ready to settle down. And, when I met Riley, I figured the best way to prove I was ready to settle down was to come home engaged."

If only something twitched on Declan's face, but no. The man's dark eyes bored into Adam's head same as they had a few minutes ago.

"I..." Adam sucked in air. "I asked her to consider a fake engagement. She agreed, but it was all my idea. I take full blame, sir. Things got kind of out of hand."

"Do you love her?"

Wasn't that the million-dollar question? "I didn't when this idea came in my head and out my mouth, sir."

"And now?" Maybe Declan's eyebrows had inched up, just a smidge.

"I think I do, but she doesn't return it. For her it was all about a chance to disappear from the public eye and make a little extra cash."

"Love..."

Adam huffed. "What do you know about it? You married my mother, but you've never loved her. She's practically a prisoner here, so don't start telling me how marriage should be founded on love."

"Don't make assumptions about my relationship with your mother."

"Please." Adam managed to stifle the eye roll.

"It's none of your business."

"She's my mother."

"She's my wife."

It took all Adam's self-control not to explode his way down the path of this particular topic. Much as he hated to admit it, Declan was right. Mom was not a prisoner. If she wanted to leave Rockstead, she could. But Adam's hope of reinstating her at Running Creek was fading quickly, right beside his own dream of reclaiming his dad's legacy.

Declan shifted from one foot to the other. "We're talking about Riley here. I don't need to explain to you that you've screwed up everything, do I?"

Adam looked down, feeling like a five-year-old caught trying to mount the green-broke horse his dad had warned him against.

"I know, sir. I apologize."

"Some things require more than a *sorry* when you get caught."

"I can't prove to you that my conscience has been bothering me before this happened, but it was. I came back from my ride ready to release Riley and then talk to you, but she was gone."

"Easy words to say now."

"I know it looks bad, sir."

"And you call yourself a Christian, like that's some lofty thing that makes you better than the rest of us."

Adam stared at the pine boards beneath his feet. Had he come across that way? "I'm sorry, sir."

Declan scoffed. "I bet you are."

"I asked God to forgive me and help me make things right while I was out riding."

"Make things right? Do you really suppose there's a way to do that?" Declan's voice was hard. Unrelenting.

"Perhaps not with you, sir, though I will ask your forgiveness anyway. I also ask that you not punish Nathaniel and Noah or even my mother for my stupidity. It's not their fault, I acted on my own."

"Noted."

Adam scuffed his boot along the pine board. "And I mean to ask Riley to forgive me, too. I was full of myself. Decided my impulsive thought was the only way. I never expected to fall in love with her."

"Which brings us back to love. Sentimentality only makes a man weak."

"Weak? I think loving Riley makes me a better man, not a weaker one. I can see how I failed to measure up, how I failed to be the man she needed me to be." He shot a glance at his stepfather. "That's why I'd already decided not to push Riley to go through with marrying me so I could claim Running Creek. I'm not saying a pretend engagement was wise, but a sham marriage would have been a far worse decision."

"You have some strange notions of right and wrong." Declan shook his head.

"I am giving it all up now. It's in God's hands. And yours."

The man chuckled, but there was no humor. "You know I don't put much stock in God. If He and I agree on anything, it's purely a coincidence."

Adam wanted to tell his stepdad that God was bigger than happenstance. That He could bring Declan around to His way of thinking. No point in pushing the topic, though. Not now. "I understand."

"You're a liar and a cheat." Declan's tone turned conversational.

A *wannabe* cheat, but this wasn't the time to split hairs. Adam hung his head. "I know, sir."

"Interesting to see you so humble."

Another goad Adam could ignore, difficult as it was.

"What are you going to do?

Did he have a choice? Was his stepfather kicking him to the curb... or not? "Some of that is up to you, sir. But I need to find Riley and make sure she knows I've come to love her with no strings attached. I don't know if she'll still have me, but I have to try."

"Love."

Adam met his stepdad's gaze. "Yes, sir. I learned about love from my parents when I was no taller than a toad. I learned about it in Sunday school down at Creekside Fellowship. I learned that God loved me enough to send His Son to die for me. To redeem me. And I want to prove to Riley that I love her that much, too. Enough to sacrifice everything."

"If you're trying to influence me, it won't work."

"That's not why." Although he wouldn't say no to it.

Come to think of it, Declan hadn't said exactly which way he was leaning.

"Well, then, have at it." Declan pulled the door open and walked out into a dull, gray afternoon. The door swung back and clicked shut.

Adam turned into the cabin and ran both hands through his hair as he dropped to his knees in front of the leather sofa. "Oh, Lord, please forgive me and guide me. I'm in so far over my head, and I don't know how to swim in this current. But, most of all, please be with Riley. Protect her, Lord. Help her to trust You... and to love me, anyway."

Because now that she'd left the ranch, he knew she was more important to him than nearly everything. More than Running Creek. But not more than his faith and honor.

He'd lay it out for her, but it was her decision if she'd return and marry him for real. Even without a ranch to call their own.

CHAPTER TWENTY-TWO

Riley scanned the crowd surging around the baggage claim in the Santa Fe airport, while Jodie watched for her garish pink suitcase. Riley didn't own that much. Everything was in her backpack except the stuff she'd left behind in October.

Where was Mom? Maybe Dad was worse, and she couldn't leave his side. Maybe Riley and her sister would need to take the shuttle into the city. Maybe...

Riley focused on dark eyes meeting her own, and her breath hitched. Oh, no. Mom had sent Raul.

He grinned at her like a feral cat sizing up a mouse.

How had Raul managed to stay in her parents' good graces? Didn't Riley's word mean anything? Not that she'd given details, but it should have been a big clue when Riley refused to allow her mother to speak Raul's name. So, thanks, Mom. There was no other way he'd have known what flight she was on.

Riley whirled away, breaking eye contact, and collided with Jodie hoisting her monstrosity off the conveyor. Even with New Mexico's warmer weather, there was no way Jodie could go through that much clothing in a few days. Wait. Was her sister running away from Mick? Planning to stay in Santa Fe? No, she wasn't like Riley. Besides, Jodie would have required a moving truck.

"Jodie, we need out of here. Now."

Her sister's wide-eyed look caught on something behind Riley.

"Hi, Riley. Hi, Jodie. Here, let me get that." Raul reached past Riley and tugged the telescoping handle to its full length. "Really, Jodie? Bright pink?" He laughed as he shook his head. "What a blow to my masculinity."

Riley stared at him. "Why are you here?"

He kissed her cheek before she could react. "I'm happy to see you, too, sweetheart."

She had not missed Raul's mocking voice at all. What she missed was Adam. Not just his voice, but everything about him.

"You know what she meant," said Jodie. "We were expecting our mother."

"And, since it's Christmas, I was expecting Santa Claus, but here we are." He took Riley's arm.

She yanked out of his grasp. "Don't touch me."

Raul grinned. "Oh, a little testy, are we?"

"Why are you here? Seriously. Mom said she'd meet our flight."

"Your mom is consulting with the neurosurgeon. She asked me to come instead." His eyebrows wobbled upward. "She seems to think we should patch up our differences."

"Not a chance."

"My sister is engaged to a hunky cowboy now. She's out of your reach, creeper."

"Oh, is that so?" He scanned Riley with a lazy smile. "Relationships on the rebound rarely work out well."

Her dad's aide had no idea how right he was, not that Riley would ever admit it. She held up her left hand. "Adam is amazing." She wanted to call him honorable and a few other adjectives, but maybe that was laying it on too thick since she didn't plan to return to Rockstead. Dad's accident had only precipitated her departure. Too bad she'd never had a chance to say goodbye.

"Oh, Riley. You're so naive." Raul rolled his eyes, dismissing Adam in five patronizing words.

Not as naive as she had been. Adam was worth a thousand Rauls. The woman Adam finally married would be the luckiest, most treasured bride on the planet. He'd managed to make Riley feel that way even when it was all a sham. Think what he'd be like if everything were real.

Riley blinked back the emotion she was barely keeping in check. This was not how things should have gone down. Not with leaving Adam behind. Not with Raul meeting her here.

"The car's right outside." Raul pointed as he led them through the sliding glass doors into a chilly evening. Not sub-zero like she'd left behind in Montana, but not exactly balmy, either, courtesy of Santa Fe's elevation.

Did she have any choice but to go with Raul? Sure, she could make a stink and call an Uber, but was she actually in any danger with this man? Her heart certainly wasn't, not anymore. And, since Raul wanted nothing more than to rise politically, he wouldn't do anything to jeopardize a Senator's daughter.

Just in case, though... Riley tapped her mom's number. It went straight to voicemail. "Hi. How's Dad? Jodie and I just arrived. Raul's here to pick us up, so we'll see you soon." There'd be a timestamp on that, if needed.

Riley slid into the backseat of Raul's sedan, leaving Jodie to ride up front. She didn't miss Raul's low chuckle as they pulled out of the lot.

Just try something, buster. I'm not the weak girl who ran away ten weeks ago. I've learned about honor and love since then. If only Adam loved her in return.

ADAM TAPPED on the door to his mother's suite. "Mom? It's Adam." He'd seen his sisters in the living room upstairs, which was perfect. He didn't want to air everything in front of the twins.

"Come in, son."

He breathed a prayer as he nudged the door open.

Ezra leaped off Mom's lap from where she sat in her gray armchair, cocooned with a fuzzy blanket and her slippered feet propped on the ottoman.

Adam bent to ruffle the small dog's ears then straightened to take in his mother's face. Her eyes were brighter than they'd been in a while. Too bad he was here to undermine her interest in life. He took a deep breath as he sank to the sofa across from her.

"Merry Christmas, son."

He removed his hat and lowered his head, rubbing both hands through his short hair. "Riley's gone."

"But just to see her father, right?"

"I don't think so. She took everything with her and left me a note."

"But... I don't understand. Just yesterday, she..."

"I know." Adam swallowed hard. "I have a confession to make."

When his mom didn't reply, he glanced up to see her head tipped to one side, an inscrutable expression on her face.

"It was all a sham, Mom. I wanted to push Declan. I thought he'd be more likely to let the twins and me have Running Creek if I were engaged. I wanted to get you out of here, too. I had lots of noble reasons."

"A... sham?"

"I'd just met Riley. She needed a place to lie low for a bit. I needed... a fake fiancée. We agreed to help each other for a few months."

"Oh, Adam."

"I'm sorry, Mom. I'm sorry I lied to you. Lied to everyone."

"First, let me get one thing clear. I don't need your help with my husband, son. I have reasons for being here you could not possibly understand."

"Try me."

"No. It has nothing to do with you."

Adam ground his teeth in frustration. "But you're sad all the time."

"I don't need your help."

How could that possibly be? Was his mom faking

depression for some reason all her own? If that were true, and she really loved Declan, why play around? Why not grab happiness with both hands?

That's what Adam should do. Grab happiness.

"Now that we've cleared the air on that topic, back to Riley. You may think it was a pretense, son, but you're fooling yourself."

What? Adam's head came up, and he stared at his mom.

She gave a small smile. "I've watched you together for more than two months. If you didn't love her at the beginning, you do now. And the same is true of Riley. She loves you, Adam."

"But... no." Mom couldn't be right. Could she?

"Listen to me. A mother knows these things. I've watched how you can't take your eyes off of her. I've watched the ways your hands reach for hers, and hers for yours. I've watched her face soften when she talks about you. Once or twice might be acting, but day in and day out for months? I don't think so."

"But it's too late." The words in Riley's note spooled through his mind. *Saying goodbye now... Best this way...*

"Is she married to someone else?"

Just the thought flailed at Adam's heart like a riding whip. He shook his head.

"Then tell her." Mom sighed and relaxed deeper into her chair.

He'd been itching to book a flight to Santa Fe for several hours now, but he'd talked himself down. If Riley wanted to leave him, he couldn't hold her back. But if her father was seriously injured... and Adam loved her... shouldn't he be by her side? Did she want him there?

Did she love him back?

There was nothing in her farewell note to say so, other than the little heart over the i in her name, but that didn't mean anything. Still, there'd been the way he'd caught her looking at him sometimes. The tender way she'd held him when he grieved Ace. So many little things.

"I've messed up." Adam ran his hands through his hair. "And Declan knows everything. I won't see Running Creek for a decade at least."

"You did a foolish thing."

He flinched. "God has been poking at my conscience the whole time. I convinced myself it was for the greater good. For Nathaniel and Noah. For you—"

"We've covered that."

"I know. I'm sorry." So very sorry.

"You're forgiven. You say you've spoken to your stepfather. But have you confessed your sin to God? Because He is faithful and just to forgive you. Nothing is too big for Him to handle."

He nodded. "I had a long talk with God this morning. That's where I was when Riley found out about her dad and left with Nathaniel."

"Then pray some more until God gives you guidance."

Adam pulled to his feet. "I've lost Running Creek, haven't I? Declan didn't say for sure, but he's quite unhappy with me."

His mother shook her head. "We'll talk. But first, I'll pray. Now go."

He heaved a big sigh and bent to kiss her cheek. "Thanks, Mom. I love you."

"Tell Riley that."

Yeah. He'd like to say those words. Could he really follow her to New Mexico? He had her phone number, even though he'd had precious few chances to use it with no cell coverage on Rockstead. Maybe he'd wait until he landed to call her, though, in case she'd tell him no.

He let himself out of his mother's suite into the darkened basement hallway and closed the door. A shadow lunged.

"You're an idiot," came his brother's harsh voice.

And then Nathaniel's fist collided with Adam's chin.

RILEY HADN'T BEEN COMPLETELY PREPARED to see her dad's still form hooked up to a bunch of tubes, wires, and monitors. His thinning hair lay disheveled in sharp contrast to the neatly tucked bedding. She'd never seen his skin so sallow.

Mom led her and Jodie back out to the waiting room. Raul wasn't there, to Riley's relief.

Jodie pressed her hands together as she took a seat. "Did the police catch the other driver?"

"They have him in custody." Mom glanced at Riley. "It was Johnny Sanderson."

Oh, no. "Maggie's father? How could it be someone we know?"

Mom twisted a tissue into knots and shook her head.

Riley jerked to her feet and paced the small room. Dad. Raul. The teen girls Riley had mentored last fall, like Maggie's sister. The men she'd trusted... Dad had managed to take credit for her program. He'd do nearly anything to get reelected. Raul was even worse, playing Dad against Johnny. He'd managed to undermine her. Anything to look good to Dad and the county commissioners, led by Johnny Sanderson. Anything to launch Raul's own bid next election year.

That's why he'd proposed to Riley back in August, so that his name would start appearing in the news. It had worked. Their engagement photos had been splashed across the entertainment pages of the Santa Fe New Mexican and the Santa Fe Reporter. They'd even been showcased on TV news. At the time, Riley wondered at the coverage, but she hadn't realized Raul was leveraging every avenue to become a household name. Linked to Ernest Dunning, sure, but only as a stepping-stone for his own means.

Suave, smooth, ambitious Raul Garcia didn't care who he stomped on as he climbed the ladder, since he didn't plan on coming back down. If only she could topple him.

Did it really matter? Weren't the voters smart enough to see through his great smile? If they weren't, didn't they deserve what they got?

And, most importantly, had Johnny Sanderson ramming her father's car really been an accident?

CHAPTER TWENTY-THREE

"Get away from me," hissed Riley as Raul crowded her shoulder on the way out of the hospital the next morning. Why couldn't he just back off?

A few seconds later, she focused on the news cameras and microphones pointed her way. Oh, so that's why a smiling Raul was at her side. She stopped in the middle of the automatic door and pinned him with a glare. "You set this up."

"Set what up?"

His innocent grin didn't fool her for a second. "You really want cameras here? Because I might have a lot to say."

"Your dad's reelection hangs in the balance."

"I'm not on his staff." She shoved a finger at the center of Raul's chest. "That's on you. And you're not playing fair."

He caught her finger and leaned in to brush a kiss on her cheek. "Don't look now, but they're taking photos for the noon news."

Riley placed both hands on his chest and shoved. He stumbled backward as she turned to the cameras.

"Ms. Dunning! Can you give us any word on your father's recovery?"

"He seems to be out of danger." Riley scanned for a gap in the reporters, but they stood shoulder to shoulder.

Raul's arm slid around her waist. "Senator Dunning is expected to fully recover. Please excuse my fiancée. All this has been very traumatizing."

Riley stepped closer to the nearest camera. "I am no longer engaged to Raul Garcia. He's a lying, ch—"

"Like I said. Very distraught." Raul lifted her left hand to a reporter. "And definitely engaged. Now, if you'll excuse us, we're headed over to the police station to learn more about the *accident*."

Several cameras were aimed directly at Riley's hand. "This is not Raul's ring I'm wearing. We broke up months ago, because he—"

"Excuse us." Raul's voice cut through hers.

Riley yanked away from him and stalked over to one of the other cameras. "Hear me. Mr. Garcia is not to be trusted. I'm engaged to a cowboy in Montana." Would any of the national channels pick up this altercation? She could only hope, but that hope dissipated in two seconds flat. Adam didn't watch the news. He was too busy. Too absorbed in the daily life of Rockstead Ranch to worry about political machinations in other states, even if his ex-fake-fiancée was embroiled in them.

It was crazy when her best hope was Mrs. McDiarmid seeing the news and gossiping about it to Adam.

A microphone was thrust in Riley's face. "Tell us where you've been since you left Santa Fe. Why did you go?"

Raul's fingers tightened around her bicep. "Riley..." The warning in his voice was unmistakable.

She pivoted toward him, unsteady as he tried to propel her past the reporter. "Let go of me. I am not going anywhere with you."

"Darling—"

If only she could get a fist free, she'd *darling* him right back, but his hands pinned her arms to her side. Not in a way that likely looked threatening. Just possessive. Supporting.

Why didn't someone rescue her? All the cameras were filming. Best news story of the day. Probably of the year, but no one would interfere.

Raul leaned into the microphone. "As you can see, Ms. Dunning is beside herself with anxiety over her father, and we have a few things to work through. We'll get a statement to you later. Excuse us." He propelled her toward a gap forming between reporters. His sedan wasn't far beyond.

Once in the car, he wouldn't be as pleasant as yesterday when he still thought he could bully her. When Jodie had been with them. There was no way she was getting in a closed space with him again.

She dug the heels of her worn cowboy boots against the edge of the sidewalk and jerked loose from him. "Did you send Johnny Sanderson to ram my dad?"

A distraction. That's all she'd meant it to be, but a cloud of fury crossed his face as he grabbed at her again. "You don't know anything, little girl." His voice was low.

Undoubtedly too low for the reporters behind them to pick up.

A fist flashed past her head and rammed into Raul's face. Her ex staggered back, blood spurting from his nose, then the rage turned to ice, and he rushed her.

Riley lunged aside but managed to leave her boot in Raul's path. He tripped over it and right into her rescuer.

Adam!

She gasped, but he was busy. His next punch landed low in Raul's gut, doubling the creep over.

"Call 9-1-1, woman."

Good idea. She fumbled her phone out of her hip pocket and tapped the number.

"We've got all that on record." A cameraman stood over her, his long lens pointed at Raul on the ground with Adam twisting his arm behind his back.

"You won't get away with this!" gasped Raul.

"Don't pretend you gave Riley that diamond. Don't pretend you have any claim over her." Adam applied a little more pressure to Raul's wrist. "She's free to choose whomever she loves, and it won't be you."

Riley's heart leaped then stuttered. He'd come all this way to acknowledge that she had the right to let him go? But she didn't want Adam free. She wanted him wrapped up in her arms, loving her like she meant the world to him.

His gaze caught on hers for a few seconds, but then a police officer elbowed in, dragged Raul upright, and snapped handcuffs on his wrists. Another officer pulled Adam aside and held him back. "What's going on here?"

"I've got it all on tape, sir," the reporter said. "Mr.

Garcia seemed to be abducting Ms. Dunning until this man stepped in. I'm happy to share the footage."

"I'm bleeding!" whined Raul. Red spattered his white shirt.

Riley dared to breathe. But, when she met Adam's intense gaze, she almost forgot how again.

"You're all coming with us." The officer gave Riley a hard look. "You, too, Ms. Dunning."

"Yes, sir. I do have one thing to say, though."

"Speak."

She turned to the reporter. "Thank you."

"No problem, ma'am. What he did to you didn't look right to me."

"It wasn't right. You know why?" She looked right into the camera, hoping it was still recording. "Because this man who came to my rescue? He's the Montana cowboy I told you about. His name is Adam Cavanagh. I love him, and I intend to marry him."

It took a couple of hours for Adam and Riley to be released. More turned out to be at stake than Adam's altercation with Riley's ex. The slimeball had tried to cover over his reaction to Riley's accusation about hiring Sanderson, but it had been caught on record. His rebuttal hadn't held water for long. Especially not after a detective visited Mr. Sanderson's jail cell and asked a few pointed questions about his relationship to Mr. Garcia.

They were free to go.

Raul Garcia was not.

Adam ushered Riley outside the police station. He grasped Riley's hand tightly in his own as though she were about to disappear again. After her words into the camera, he was pretty sure she wouldn't, but he didn't want to let go. Not now. Not ever.

Riley looked up at him and touched his cheek with a featherlight finger. "Did Raul give you that bruise?"

"Uh, no. My brother decked me."

She pulled back, her eyes wide. "*What?*"

"Nathaniel. After he got back from driving you to the airport. He had a few choice things to say about how I'd been treating you."

"You treated me just fine."

Adam had to love her loyalty. He cradled her face between his hands and brushed his lips lightly against hers. "Did you mean what you said to the reporter?"

"Depends on what you're referring to."

That might be a gleam in her eyes.

He held her gaze. "That you love me. For real."

"I do. It might not be wise of me."

Adam's gut tightened. "Why wouldn't it be?"

"Because we've both been pretending for so long, I don't know what's truth anymore." Her eyes searched his. "And because you might not feel the same."

His fingers tangled in her unruly hair. "What if I told you..." He trailed kisses across her face. "What if I told you I loved you more than anyone or anything in the world, but it might not be wise of you to love me back?"

"Why wouldn't it be?" she whispered, echoing him.

"Because I told Declan everything. He hasn't come right out and said it, but I'm certain I've lost Running Creek.

Nathaniel hates my guts, while Noah is only severely disappointed. I made my mother cry. I'm a loser, Riley. I have nothing to offer you except my love and devotion, but I promise that's yours forever."

Riley held his wrists where he touched her face. That brash diamond gleamed on the ring finger of her left hand. He'd bought it for show, but now it didn't seem big enough — bold enough — to declare his love.

Then she stretched the distance between them and melded her mouth to his.

Adam stilled his breath as he closed his eyes, accepting her kiss for a long moment before he groaned and gathered her close. "Oh, Riley. I love you so much. I don't know why you love me back, but I'm thankful."

"Because you're a man of integrity," she whispered between kisses. "Because you follow Jesus."

He'd done a poor job of that. "But I used you for my own advancement."

"I used you, too, to get away from Raul, though I never dreamed he was capable of this. But I knew what I was getting in for with you. You never lied to me, Adam. Not once."

No. No, he hadn't. But he'd listened to the rumors. "Scotty..."

"I've never felt a thing for him. Since the moment I met you, it's been *you*, all the way, every day."

"You believe in love at first sight?" It had taken him longer, but man, the attraction had sure been there from the first kiss. He'd desperately needed to keep her in his life. Keep her close. Even if he'd gone about it the wrong way.

"Maybe?"

Her phone dinged, and Riley sighed before pulling it from her pocket and thumbing it on. Then she smiled. "Dad's awake."

"He's going to be okay?"

"I think so."

"I should get you back to the hospital. Sorry, my rental car is over there, so we'll need to get an Uber." He hesitated. "Do you want lunch first? I have no idea what time it is."

"We can get something in the cafeteria later. Or a vending machine." She linked her hand with his and swung them together. "Am I dreaming? Because I like this dream."

"Did you miss the part where I'm unemployed?"

"Did *you* miss the part where it doesn't matter? We'll figure it all out. Together."

"I don't deserve you." Yes, he'd come all this way to declare himself, but he'd never dreamed she'd take him back before he was done groveling. He'd never dreamed she'd take him back at all. That she'd loved him all along. Why had he been so blind?

"None of us deserves grace, Adam. God has forgiven me so much. I know your heart was in the right place." She fingered the collar of his shirt. The shirt she'd given him.

She wore the necklace and earrings, too. He'd only just noticed. The most important gift she wore was his ring.

Adam lifted her left hand and pressed a kiss to her knuckles. "This ring... I'd rather you didn't pawn it, Ry."

"Oh?" She smiled up at him, her head tilted to one side. "Why's that?"

"Because I'd like to authenticate that rash proposal."

"Why, Adam." She batted her eyelashes. "It's like you want to marry me for real, cowboy. Is that what you're saying?"

Hope, joy, and love bubbled over in his heart. "Are you proposing to me, woman?"

"Would you say yes if I were?"

He crushed his lips against hers, claiming her, branding her. "I say yes. I love you, Ry."

CHAPTER TWENTY-FOUR

Jodie towed Riley to a corner of the waiting room, her eyes wide as she glanced toward Adam sitting with their mother. "I thought you were making him up!"

Riley shook her head. "He's very real." Even though their relationship hadn't been.

"He's gorgeous. And hot!" Jodie fanned her face.

He was rather. "I told you what happened." In two minutes or less, but Riley owed her sister and parents the complete story soon.

"You told me, yeah, but I'd grab a man like him, too, and never let go."

Riley laughed. "Keep your hands off Adam."

"Oh, for your sake, I will. And I wouldn't stand a chance, anyhow."

"Besides, you've got Mick..."

Jodie gritted her teeth. "About him."

"Yeah?"

"He's a jerk."

Riley searched her sister's face. "What's going on?"

"I'm pregnant. I thought he'd be happy. All he wanted to know was how I could keep working to support him with a baby."

"Oh, no."

"We had a deal, he said. But then he went to a Christmas party without me — since I wouldn't drink — and hooked up with some other girl."

Riley folded her arms around her sister. "I'm so sorry. Are you going to be all right?"

"I'm going to stay here with Mom and Dad for a bit while I figure things out. I can help take care of Dad once they release him."

"That sounds like a good solution. Shouldn't be too long, right? They're moving him out of ICU today."

"How long are you sticking around?"

"A couple of days, I think. Adam needs to get back to Montana for a wedding on New Year's Eve. His best friend from his rodeo days is getting married."

Adam had sounded genuinely happy for Sawyer and Anna, even though their story had been mighty rocky, too. It didn't sound like Mick would pursue Jodie and their baby the way Sawyer had pursued Anna.

"Men just use women to get what they want." Jodie's voice was low. "And women put up with it, like Mom has."

"That's what I've always thought, too. Remember the way they used to fight and then pretend nothing was wrong in public?"

Jodie shuddered. "Do I ever."

"After the mess Adam and I made over things, I can understand it more. They were sticking together for the sake of us girls as well as Dad's career. I thought Mom was weak for buckling under, but she made a decision she felt was right. And, somehow, they love each other."

Was the same thing true for Kathryn and Declan? Adam had told her how upset his mom had been at his attempts to fix things for her, that she didn't need his help. Riley's parents didn't need her help, either. Her prayers? For sure. But not her help.

A movement by the entrance to the unit caught Riley's attention. The door swung open and a nurse emerged towing a gurney. "Family of Mr. Dunning? He's on his way to a private room out on the floor."

Riley crossed the space and grasped her dad's hand. "You're looking good." At least, a whole lot better than yesterday.

He offered her a wan smile but his eyes searched the room until Mom stepped up beside them. She leaned over and kissed his cheek. "Riley's right, Ernie. We're all glad to see your progress."

Riley exchanged a smile with her sister. Maybe there was hope for their parents yet. No one had told Dad about Raul, though. He needed to get stronger before they lobbed that one at him. He'd mentored Raul. Trusted him. Encouraged Riley to marry him.

Adam's hands settled on Riley's hips from behind, and she leaned back against him. He nuzzled her ear. "I love you."

This cowboy. He was much more to her liking.

He clasped her hand as they fell into step behind the gurney, with Jodie on her other side.

She couldn't wait to see what their future would hold. Together.

HIS BEST FRIEND'S New Year's Eve wedding took place in the expansive lower level at Eaglecrest, with a casual reception upstairs before Sawyer and Anna drove off in a black truck festooned with streamers. Fireworks sent the newlyweds off with a bang, to the delight of the children who were present.

Adam held his beloved close in the shadows as the other guests trooped back toward the house, laughing and talking. The door closed behind the small crowd, leaving Adam and Riley alone in the sub-zero night. Bright stars dotted the moonless night.

She melted against him. "Wow, Sawyer's mom pulled that together in just one week?"

"Crazy, right?" Nothing had looked like a hasty afterthought, that was for sure. Made Adam wonder how quickly they could put their own wedding together at Rockstead. Except his mom and stepdad didn't work together like Russ and Gloria Delgado. And there was the minor matter of the way Adam and Declan had left the situation between them.

Adam's heart sank. A wedding like this one could give a guy hope and fill his mind with possibilities, but Sawyer hadn't spent months living a lie that had just come into the open. No, since the moment he'd discovered Anna was carrying his child, he'd pursued her openly and with single-minded determination.

Nothing underhanded like Adam had done. Would Declan ever forgive him? Riley's parents had, but the lie hadn't been for their benefit to start with.

Several families exited the house, piled into their vehicles, and drove away.

"We should go in and see if we can be of use with the cleanup." Adam's thoughts were heavy.

"It was good of Delgados to offer us a place to stay tonight."

"It was." The house was nearly as large as Rockstead. Plenty big enough to take in a few strays. Most of the other guests lived in nearby Saddle Springs.

"Adam?"

"What, my love?"

"It will be okay. Really."

He kissed her then, long and hard, before tugging her toward the house. After they'd shed their outerwear, they entered the kitchen where Russ, a hand towel slung over his shoulder, loaded the dishwasher while Gloria packed leftovers into containers.

Russ glanced between Adam and Riley with a knowing smile. "So glad you two could make it. I know it meant a lot to Sawyer."

Adam chuckled. "As if he even noticed." The man's eyes had been riveted to his bride.

"Oh, he noticed, all right. How are things at Rockstead?"

This was the opening Adam had been waiting for. "I'm not sure, sir. I did something very foolish, telling my stepfather Riley and I were engaged when it wasn't true. I was trying to push him into handing over my dad's ranch to my brothers and me, but it backfired when he found out it was all a ruse."

Russ pushed the dishwasher closed. He rested both hands on the island countertop as he studied Adam. "But it's true now."

Riley's hand slipped into his, and Adam grasped it gratefully. "Absolutely true. We had a rocky start, but Riley and I are on the right track now. We've forgiven each other. God's forgiven us. The only problem is my stepfather."

"I see."

Adam took a deep breath. "I'm looking for work, and I'm wondering if you could use another hand here at Eaglecrest. I've given up hope of reconciliation. Pretty sure I've lost all Declan's respect forever."

Looking at him pensively, Gloria shifted over beside Russ.

"I'd understand if you didn't want me around."

"Oh, Adam, that's not it at all." Gloria shook her head. "We've all done wrong. So many blunders. But if we repent, God forgives us. Then how can humans keep holding onto grievance?"

She obviously hadn't met Declan Cavanagh.

Russ glanced at his wife. "My first instinct is that you should stay at Rockstead. Your stepdad needs to see your steadfastness. Your willingness to work and do the right thing. We'll pray with you. I'm sure God can change his heart and bring him around."

Even though it gutted him to give up what his dad had worked for, it would be so much easier to wash his hands of Rockstead and Running Creek forever. "Declan told me flat out that if he and God saw eye-to-eye on anything, it would be a coincidence."

"Don't you think God is bigger than that show of bravado?"

Good question. Obvious answer. Adam took a deep breath. "You're right. God can perform a miracle."

Sawyer's parents exchanged another look then Russ turned back to Adam. "No doubt you're entering calving season over there soon as we are here at Eaglecrest. Pray hard, Adam. Work hard. And if, in a few months, Declan is still set against you, let me know. We'll work something out then if needed."

A weight lifted off Adam's heart. "Thank you, sir. You don't know what this means to me."

"And me," put in Riley.

Gloria grinned at Riley. "So, when's the big day? If you need any help planning a wedding, I'm all yours. I can't believe our own boys are all married off now."

Adam squeezed Riley's fingers. "We're talking around Easter. It looks like Riley's dad will have recovered enough to travel by then, but we need to check the dates our church in Jewel Lake has open." Wasn't Mrs. McDiarmid going to love this?

"Well, I hope we're invited."

"Absolutely."

IT HAD BEEN a whole lot easier to talk to Russ and Gloria than Declan and Kathryn. For one thing, the senior Delgados had stood side by side like partners, unlike the

Cavanaghs. Declan looked totally out of his element at the end of the gray sofa, while Kathryn sat in her usual armchair with Ezra curled up on her lap. The Yorkie wasn't asleep, though. He was watchful.

Riley and Adam had dropped to cushions on the floor. It was either that or sit next to Declan, and the sofa didn't seem long enough. Besides, then he'd be harder to see. Harder to read.

Not that Riley could discern thoughts or emotions on the man's face anyway.

Declan leaned onto his knees, staring between them. "You wanted to talk to your mother and me, so talk."

Riley slid her hand into Adam's for moral support.

Adam's chin came up slightly. "I've asked Riley to marry me, and she said yes."

Declan's eyebrows shot up. "If you think this is going to sway me..."

"That's not why, sir. I've made a lot of mistakes in the past few months. I've already confessed them to you and to God—"

"Get to the point." Declan's hand chopped through the air.

"Riley and I love each other. It took us a while to realize it after our rocky start, but we do. We want to spend the rest of our lives together, not for the purpose of gaining Running Creek, but because we can't imagine life without each other. I've just gotten off the phone with the Creek-side Fellowship secretary—"

"That busybody, Melanie McDiarmid."

"She means well," murmured Riley.

Declan shook his head.

"Anyway, we've booked the church and hall for the first Saturday in April. We hope you'll be happy for us."

"If you think it changes anything, you're mistaken." Declan surged to his feet. "It will take more than that to prove yourself to me after all you've said and done."

Adam stood and faced his stepfather. "I understand, sir. I'd like to keep working for you, if you're willing to have me. To have us. It's up to you."

"I could use you around for calving."

He'd give Adam all the night shifts in the barn, no doubt.

Declan glanced at his wife then back at Adam. "Your mother and I will discuss this later. Meanwhile, have a look at the yearlings in the west pen. Some of them look a little listless."

"Yes, sir. I've got a bit more to say to Mom before we go."

Declan shrugged and went out.

"Mom..."

"Don't start, Adam." She smiled at Riley. "I'm happy to welcome you into this family, disjointed as it seems to be. Tell me what you're thinking for the wedding."

Adam tugged her over to the newly vacated sofa, and she took a seat beside him. "Well, Adam wants to have Noah and Nathaniel stand up for him."

Kathryn nodded, smiling.

"I have one sister, Jodie. She'll be my maid of honor." Riley hesitated. Was anyone ready for her other choice? She doubted it. "And I'd like to ask Dakota as well."

"Dakota Erickson?" Adam pulled away, staring at her. "Are you serious?"

"Totally. She's the closest thing I have to a friend around here, and I'd like to think this might cement our friendship."

"I'm not sure—"

"I think it's a great idea," interrupted Kathryn. "I'm glad to see you're willing to be her friend. Lord willing, she and Travis will get things worked out yet."

Adam studied Riley's face, and she looked up at him, waiting. "You're sure?"

"I am."

He brushed a kiss over her lips. "Whatever makes you happy, then. So long as there are no surprises in the groom department."

"None at all. I'm going to marry you for real, cowboy. Get ready for it."

His intense gaze warmed her to the core. "Oh, I'm ready, woman."

And so was she.

EPILOGUE

What's Mama doing?" Toby wiggled his bony backside back and forth on Travis's leg as he stared toward the front of the sanctuary. The entire platform was bedecked with flowers and candles, providing a backdrop for a grand ceremony. Travis's step-brother's wedding.

How had Dakota finagled her way into the wedding party? It was like she'd betrayed Travis all over again, picking the other side. It must be because he was so easy to leave. His mom had been the first. She hadn't tossed him a backward glance on her way out the door. Dakota wouldn't have, either, if they didn't share custody of Toby. No way was Travis giving up access to his son.

Toby slammed his head hard against Travis's chest. That was gonna leave a bruise. "What's Mama *doing?*" His voice was louder this time.

"Shh. We're in church."

"But *what?*"

A few people tittered. Alexia twisted around in the front pew and scowled at the four-year-old and then, pointedly, at Travis. Of course, his teenage sisters warranted seats of honor between Dad and Kathryn. Adam was their half-brother, but Travis, Blake, and Ryder barely rated second-tier status for the day.

Travis sighed and pressed his finger against his son's mouth. Hadn't they gone over this before the ceremony started? "Your mama is helping Adam and Riley get married," he whispered.

The only good thing about today was watching Dakota without anyone noticing. It had been a long time since she'd dressed to the nines for a date with him. He'd never seen her hair all done up fancy with just a few trailing curls brushing her shoulders. In a flirty dress like this one, pale pink with a deep V in the back. She went more for the urban cowgirl look most of the time.

Toby bopped his skull back against Travis's chest enough times that Travis tightened his hold around the little guy, the only part of Dakota he had left. Once things between them had been good. Promising. Now? Not so much.

But Adam had come back from a pretty stupid mistake and still won his girl. How did the guy land on his feet time after time? Although, perhaps, not with Running Creek. So far, Travis's dad refused to clarify his stance on the Anderson ranch.

Served Adam right.

Pastor Marshall pronounced Adam and Riley husband and wife, and Travis watched them kiss for a few seconds before snapping his gaze back to Dakota.

Her eyes were on him, eyebrows raised.

Was she reading his thoughts? Seeing his regrets?

The music leaped into an energetic recessional. Beaming, the newlyweds practically bounded to the back of the church, followed by Riley's sister and Noah.

Then Dakota took Nathaniel's arm. Nathaniel leaned down to whisper something to her, and she laughed. Both of them met Travis's gaze as they swept by.

Get your hands off my woman, cowboy.

Somehow Travis kept his seat. Dakota wasn't his. Hadn't been for a long time. She was a free agent, and she made sure Travis knew it.

It killed him. Every single day.

A NOTE FROM VALERIE:

Happy sigh. Adam and Riley have earned their happily-ever-after. :)

But... Travis. Did you love to hate him? He hasn't wasted much time in his life trying to win his stepbrothers' favor, but maybe they've just misunderstood him. How much will his attitude trip him up as he tries to win back the mother of his young son? For Toby's sake, I hope his dad is ready to take action. You know Dakota's going to make him work for reconciliation, right? What's it going to take?

Read all about Travis and Dakota in
Give Me Another Chance, Cowboy.

Did you miss Sawyer and Anna's story?
Check out *The Cowboy's Reluctant Bride.*

ACKNOWLEDGMENTS

Ah, cowboys! There's just something about them, isn't there? Masculine, hardworking, resourceful, honorable, and gentlemanly... a cowboy is hard to beat.

Thank YOU, dear reader, for loving the Saddle Springs Romance series so much I was inspired to write the Cavanagh Cowboys Romance series as a spin-off. I hope you enjoy the ride. Pun intended!

Always, always, thanks to my fellow author and friend, Elizabeth Maddrey. She prods, cheers, and commiserates as needed, then offers helpful critiques and continued encouragement. If you haven't read her Christian contemporary romances, go find them and get started!

I also appreciate my beta readers: Paula, Amy, Debbie, and Joelle. These gals combed through an earlier draft of *Marry Me for Real, Cowboy* to find any errors or inconsistencies. I am forever grateful!

My amazing editor, Nicole, has been with me from the beginning. I can't give her enough kudos for her support and her eagle eye as we discuss the differences between "she was under no illusions" and "she was under no delusions..." and other tricky word choices.

I'm also grateful for the Christian Indie Authors Facebook group and my sister bloggers at Inspy Romance.

These folks make a difference in my life every single day. I'm thrilled to walk beside them as we tell stories for Jesus!

Thank you to my Facebook friends, followers, street team, and reader group members for prayers, encouragement, and great fellowship. If you'd like to join other readers who love my stories, please find us at Valerie Comer: Readers Group.

Thanks to my husband, Jim, whose love for me never fails and who encourages me in every endeavor. Thanks to my kids, their spouses, and my wonderful grandgirls for cheering me on. To them, having an author for a mom/grandma is "normal." Imagine that!

All my love and gratitude goes to Jesus, the One who is my vision, the High King of Heaven, the lord of my heart. Thank you. A thousand times, thank you.

ABOUT THE AUTHOR

Valerie Comer lives where food meets faith in her real life, her fiction, and on her blog and website. She and her husband of over 35 years farm, garden, and keep bees on a small farm in Western Canada, where they grow and preserve much of their own food.

Valerie has always been interested in real food from scratch, but her conviction has increased dramatically since God blessed her with four delightful granddaughters. In this world of rampant disease and pollution, she is compelled to do what she can to make these little girls' lives the best she can. She helps supply healthy food — local food, organic food, seasonal food — to grow strong bodies and minds.

Valerie is a *USA Today* bestselling author and a two-time Word Award winner. She is known for writing engaging characters, strong communities, and deep faith laced with humor into her green clean romances.

To find out more, visit her website www.valeriecomer.com where you can read her blog, and explore her many links. You can also find Valerie blogging with other authors of Christian contemporary romance at Inspy Romance.

Why not join her email list where you will find news, giveaways, deals, book recommendations, and more? Your thank-you gift is *Promise of Peppermint*, the prequel novella to the Urban Farm Fresh Romance series.

http://valeriecomer.com/subscribe

www.ingramcontent.com/pod-product-compliance
Lightning Source LLC
Chambersburg PA
CBHW050727180626
46814CB00002B/643